DATE		

A Snitch in the

A Snitch in the

by Julie Anne Peters

Megan Tingley Books
Little, Brown and Company
BOSTON   NEW YORK   LONDON

First Edition

The characters and events portrayed in this book are fictitious. Any
similarity to real persons, living or dead, is coincidental and not
intended by the author.

Library of Congress Cataloging-in-Publication Data

Peters, Julie Anne.
    A snitch in the Snob Squad / by Julie Anne Peters — 1st ed.
      p.   cm.
    Summary: Twelve-year-old Jenny and the other members
of the Snob Squad suspect that one of them, or someone close
to them, is behind the thefts at their school.
    ISBN 0-316-70287-0
    [1. Stealing — Fiction.   2. Schools — Fiction.   3. Weight
control — Fiction.]   I. Title.
PZ7.P44158 Sn 2001
[Fic] — dc21   00-062334

10 9 8 7 6 5 4 3 2 1

MV-NY

Printed in the United States of America

To my sister Susan,
for believing in me

A Snitch in the

Chapter 1

"**W**ow," Max said.

"Wow," I said.

"W-wow," Prairie said.

"I know." Lydia beamed. "It's awesome."

I'm not easily awed, but in this instance Lydia was right. Everyone else had used a shoebox, the way Mrs. Jonas, our homeroom teacher, had suggested. But Lydia had converted an empty corrugated case of Bounty paper towels into the biggest, coolest, most authentic-looking diorama ever constructed by a sixth grader. On this or any other planet.

"It's an exact replica of the Declaration Chamber in Independence Hall," Lydia said. "See, I even have a picture of the reconstruction." She held up the report accompanying the diorama.

"How long did that take you?" Max asked.

"Three weeks and two days," Lydia answered. "I had to hot-glue all the furniture together and paint it.

I bought the miniature chandelier, but I cut out the curtains myself. And I hand-drew all fifty-six of the Founding Fathers. See, here's John Hancock with his quill pen, signing the Declaration of Independence."

A snort sounded behind us. "You sure that's not his sister, Jane? He looks like a girl." Ashley Krupps wedged her fleshy mass between Max and me. It felt like Jabba the Hutt coming through. "In fact, they all look like girls."

Lydia curled a lip at Ashley. "The Founding Fathers were not girls, you twit. Everyone had long hair back then." Lydia rolled her eyes at us.

Really. I rolled mine back. She'd answered my question, though.

"All right, everyone, let's get settled," Mrs. Jonas called from her desk. The crowd gathered around Lydia's diorama dispersed, but the four of us, the Snob Squad, lingered for a last look. "It's s-so cool," Prairie told Lydia.

Lydia smiled. "Thanks. I really want it to be picked as our class project in social studies. You know, for the PTA's open house? My mom's running for president next year."

Which didn't surprise me. Lydia's mom was very involved in Lydia's life. She had to be — she was a child psychologist.

On the way back to our desks, I heard Ashley lean

across the aisle and say to her groupie, Melanie Mason, "She cheated. I bet her mommy helped her. No way she made that herself."

Unfortunately, Lydia was right behind me. "I did too make it myself!" she shrieked.

Everyone within earshot was immediately hearing impaired.

"Lydia, sit down," Mrs. Jonas snapped. "Will everyone just sit down and be quiet so I can take the lunch count? I have a splitting headache." Mrs. Jonas covered her forehead with her hand. She had more headaches than any teacher I'd ever known. Maybe because this was her first year teaching. Someone should've warned her.

"Raise your hands again for hot lunch," Mrs. Jonas said. As I twisted around to ask Prairie what kind of pig slop was on the menu today, I saw Hugh Torkerson blow her a kiss. Oh, brother. How corny. Unless, of course, Kevin Rooney was inclined. Speaking of my true love. . . .

Our eyes met. My stomach flip-flopped. Hard to believe Kevin was actually my sort-of boyfriend. We hadn't progressed as far in our relationship as Prairie and Hugh. No kiss-blowing. Not even hand-holding, but he had taken me to the sixth-grade spring fling and there were definitely vibes between us. Sizzling vibes.

Lydia raised her hand. "Mrs. Jonas?"

Uh-oh, I thought. When Lydia affected her whiny voice, we all knew what was coming.

"Ashley is wearing a hat, in case you hadn't noticed." Lydia lowered her hand.

Mrs. Jonas sighed. "Ashley?"

"Oh, come on, Mrs. Jonas. It's two weeks till school's out. Can't we have a little bit of freedom?"

Mrs. Jonas said, "It's not my rule. It's the school's."

Ashley cocked her head. "My father won't care. Ask him."

Nobody needed to ask. Everybody knew that the rules didn't apply to Ashley Krupps, the principal's prima donna daughter. Mrs. Jonas pushed herself up from her desk chair like it hurt to move. "Take out your daily oral language," she said wearily.

"You wouldn't let any of *us* wear hats." Lydia's voice rose. "Last time Max wore her Pennzoil cap, you confiscated it and wrote her up."

All eyes zoomed in on Max. She spit a sunflower seed shell into her desk and looked bored.

Lydia went on, "Why do you always let Ashley get away with murder?"

A rhetorical question, if ever I heard one. Just to goad Lydia, Ashley reached inside her desk and pulled out a half-empty Bonus Pak of Cinn*A*Burst gum. She handed a stick to Melanie and unwrapped one for herself.

"Mrs. Jonas!" Lydia screeched, pointing.

I sent her a silent plea: Just drop it, Lydia. Life isn't fair. So what else is new?

"Now they're chewing gum again. It's not just Ashley. Melanie gets special treatment, too."

"Oh, and you don't?" Ashley exploded. "Who gets extra recess time for cleaning the boards and tidying up the art cabinet? Who gets to be the room monitor like every day? Who gets extra credit for sucking up to every teacher in this school?"

Mrs. Jonas whirled. Her face was scarlet. Between clenched teeth, she said, "I'll see both of you at lunchtime. Now shut up and open your DOL."

I shrank in my seat. Mrs. Jonas yelled a lot, but she'd never said, "Shut up." Hooboy. By the end of the school year everyone was always a little testy. Except the teachers. We counted on them to keep us from killing each other.

Poor Mrs. Jonas. She looked like she was ready to barf. If she did, I hoped the chunks would fly as far as Ashley's fat face.

We all hated Ashley Krupps. Any self-respecting person would. But Ashley wasn't the most unpopular person at Montrose Middle School. That honor was shared by the four of us, the Snob Squad: Max, Prairie, Lydia, and me, Jenny Solano. We weren't really snobs; just thrived on the notoriety. You could say we had

Ashley Krupps to thank for our friendship, since it was our mutual loathing of her that had brought us together.

You'd never hear Lydia thank Ashley — for anything. Following her meeting with Mrs. Jonas, Lydia stormed into the cafeteria and slammed her lunch tray on the table. She jammed in beside me on the bench and snarled, "I despise her. I detest her. I spit on her slimy guts."

Prairie, Max, and I exchanged cautious glances. Since I was the leader of the Snob Squad, it was my duty to ask, "So, what happened?"

"What do you think happened?!" Lydia screeched, puncturing my eardrum. "The same thing that always happens. Somebody else gets in trouble for something Ashley did. In this case, me." Lydia ripped open a carton of milk. She took a swig from the wedge, swallowed, and set the carton down so hard milk sloshed out. "Mrs. Jonas is the worst teacher in the world," she said. "Do you know after she ragged on Ashley and me for being disruptive, she actually let Ashley stay in the room to eat her lunch? *We* never get to eat in the room."

Out the cafeteria door, I saw Mrs. Jonas at the drinking fountain, knocking down a handful of aspirin. "Two more weeks, Lyd." I patted her sharp shoulder blade. "Just two more weeks."

"Of total living hell," she muttered.

"What other kind is there?" Max said.

We all looked at her. Max was a person of few words, but when she spoke, it was profound.

"Let's change the subject," I said. "This is giving me indigestion."

As if on cue, Kevin Rooney wandered by. "Hey, Jen," he said.

The lunch meat in my stomach congealed. "Hey," I said back. A brilliant conversationalist I'm not.

"You want to go shoot some hoops?" He bounced a basketball at his side. Down up, down up. It was making me queasy.

"No, that's okay," I told him. "You go ahead." It wouldn't further our relationship to have my one true love repulsed by my B.O., not to mention my fat arms flapping in the breeze.

He did a little pout. "See ya, then." He smiled. That crooked half-smile that was so adorable.

"Oh, man. You shoulda gone," Max chided me after Kevin left. "The guys never ask us to play."

"They never ask *you* to play," Lydia countered. "Why?" She answered her own question, "Because you beat the crap out of them."

Max grinned. "So true. Hey, did I tell you guys I might try out for the Junior All-Stars basketball league this summer?"

All eyes focused on Max. She rarely volunteered information about herself, which was probably a good thing. Saved us from being accomplices in her illicit activities.

Lydia said, "I didn't know we had a girls' all-star league."

Max bit into her hamburger and garbled, "Who said it was girls?"

We gaped. At least, I did. Don't ask me why. Max was an awesome athlete. Unlike the rest of us, who were safer on the sidelines.

"That's really smart, Max." Lydia's eyes gleamed. "My mom's always telling me I should play more sports if I want to meet boys."

I blinked at her. "Is that why she's making you take ballet?"

"No." Lydia clucked her tongue. "She says ballet will improve my coordination. So that one day I *can* play sports." She shoveled a spoonful of gray corn into her mouth.

"You'll m-make it for sure," Prairie said to Max.

Max's eyes dropped. "I said I *might* try out. It's pretty expensive. You have to buy your own uniform and equipment. I'd need better shoes, like Nike Air Zooms or Flightposites."

The only shoes I'd ever seen Max wear were her scruffy army boots. Even now, when everyone else was wearing sandals. But I guess army boots were fitting when you marched to a different drummer.

After lunch we wandered out to the common area. It was such a warm sunny day, I just wanted to kick off my sandals and lie in the grass all afternoon. Unfortunately, our jail term wasn't up yet. The playground gestapo marshaled us back to our holding cell, which in this case was one of four stuffy temporary trailers. All the sixth graders had been relegated to temps during renovation of the C wing.

I'd just laid my head on the desk to catch my usual afternoon snooze during math when a squeal like a siren split every atom in the air. "Someone sabotaged my diorama!" Lydia screeched.

Everyone scrambled to the windows where the dioramas were set up on a display table. Sure enough, all the desks and chairs inside the Declaration Chamber had been rearranged to resemble our classroom. Most of Lydia's Popsicle-stick people were standing on their heads or stuck together against the walls like they were kissing. Someone had raided the game closet and added pieces to the scene from Clue and Monopoly and Life and chess. There were cars and weapons and hotels and pawns performing unnatural acts in the aisles.

Lydia retrieved John Hancock, who was hanging

from the clock tower by a rubber band. Her teeth clenched. She gathered up a bunch of the other stick people and thrust them out for viewing. "Look," she said. "Mustaches on all the Founding Fathers." She licked her finger and tried to wash one off. "In permanent ink." Lydia's eyes filled with tears.

Mrs. Jonas squeezed through the crowd. She lifted Lydia's limp wrist and examined John Hancock. Whirling on us, she asked, "Who did this?"

As if in slow motion, we all pivoted ninety degrees. To face Ashley, who was bent over the book rack, heaving with laughter.

Mrs. Jonas snatched John Hancock out of Lydia's hand. "To the office," she ordered. "Both of you."

At the trailer door, Mrs. Jonas paused. "Jenny," she said, pointing, "you're in charge."

I jumped. Me? In charge?

As the door slammed behind them, I cleared my throat. "Uh, okay everyone. Listen up." About a billion eyeballs bounced off my body. Which made it swell in size.

I could play this two ways. Be responsible. Be popular. Some choice. "Free time," I announced.

While everyone trashed the classroom, Prairie, Max, and I tried to unsabotage Lydia's diorama. Except for the mustaches on the girls — er, Founding

Fathers — we managed to put most of the Chamber back together.

"Here they come," Kevin whispered urgently from his lookout position at the door.

"Sit down and shut up!" I hollered.

The door flew open and Lydia stomped in, followed by Mrs. Jonas and Ashley. Lydia splat into her desk, fuming. It wouldn't have surprised me if her seat burst into flames. The smirk on Ashley's face spoke volumes.

A whole bottle of aspirin wasn't going to help Mrs. Jonas now, the way she looked. Luckily, the final bell rang. "Class dismissed." She waved feebly. "Oh, Lydia," she called as Lydia charged for the door. "If you want to come in tomorrow before school to work on your diorama, I'll be here." Under her breath, Mrs. Jonas muttered, "If I'm not in Bellevue by then."

Lydia paused at the exit. In measured steps, she walked over to the window display. She picked up her diorama and lifted it over her head. Then she threw it across the room and said, "That's what you can do with your stupid diorama."

Chapter 2

Dear Food Diary,

For lunch I ate an Oscar Mayer turkey bologna sandwich, which tastes nothing like turkey or bologna. I even ate the crust on both slices of light Wonder bread. I'm still wondering how they can get away with calling that bread. The Libby's fruit cup is for people without teeth, so for dessert I finished off Prairie's brownie. Everyone else had hot lunch: hamburgers and fries and corn and brownies.

How did I feel? Cheated.

It actually made me feel better to write it down. Ashley and I had one thing in common: We were fat. The difference between us was that I cared. I was trying to do something about my weight.

Still, keeping a food diary was the dumbest idea in the world. How was writing down everything I ate, when I ate it, why I ate it, and how I felt afterward going to help me lose twenty pounds in two weeks? Unless I got writer's cramp and they had to amputate my arm.

"Vanessa, Jenny, hurry up," Mom yelled down the hallway. "Your father has dinner ready and we have to leave."

I shoved my food diary under my pillow and rolled off the bed. The sound of muffled clarinet music wafted under my sister's bedroom door. I pounded as I passed. Don't ask me why. When Vanessa was lost in her music, the world could end in a flash flood and she'd be like, "Hey, don't get my instrument wet."

"Is Vanessa coming?" Mom asked, hurriedly pouring milk into our glasses at the kitchen table.

"What do you think?" I cupped my ear.

"Vanessa!" Mom shouted. She pleaded hopelessly at Dad with her eyes. He sighed and took off his apron before tromping down the hall. Our nightly ritual.

Mom transferred dinner from the oven to the table. Dad had done himself proud. Corn dogs and onion rings. Fried food heaven.

As I was reaching for the longest, thickest corn dog, Mom clenched my wrist and said, "I made you something special." She set a plate in front of me with a scoop of cottage cheese on it, topped by half a canned pear. Sticking out either side of the scoop were two sesame seed breadsticks.

"Think of it as Chinese gourmet." Mom smiled. "And these are the chopsticks."

I didn't say what I was thinking, which was where she could stick her chops.

Dad returned with Vanessa in tow and we all took our places. Vanessa eyed my dinner and drooled. A ninety-nine point nine percent DNA match would not prove to me that Vanessa and I were related. She was tall and skinny and talented, while I was ... Well, just picture the opposite. We did share one behavior trait: We both had addictive personalities. Vanessa was borderline anorexic and addicted to the clarinet. I was a junk food junkie and addicted to Kevin Rooney.

"Jenny, did you remember to write down everything you ate today?" Mom smiled as she squeezed a glob of ketchup onto her plate.

I glowered in response.

Van began to scrape the cornmeal off her corn dog and said, "How about the Ding Dongs you have hidden in your drawer?"

I picked up a breadstick and broke it in half, indicating the technique I would later use on her scrawny neck.

"Vanessa, stop doing that and eat your corn dog."

Mom clucked her tongue. To me, she said, "Are you hoarding food in your room again? I thought I told you —"

"I'm not hoarding food," I snapped at her. Then I added, "That was Vanessa's idea of a joke." Ha ha, I thought. How'd she know about those Ding Dongs, anyway? Borrowing a line from Max, I muttered, "She's so funny I forgot to fart."

Dad howled.

Mom silenced him with a scowl. She exhaled a short breath and said, "So, how was your day?"

Van and I both shoveled food into our mouths.

Mom said, "Vanessa?"

She glanced up and replied, "Fine."

Mom cocked her head.

Vanessa shrugged. "It was fine. Uneventful. What do you want me to say? It was school. Duh."

Mom sighed. "And how was your day, Jenny?" She twisted my way. "Don't tell me uneventful."

I sucked up a curd of cottage cheese and gagged. Setting down my spoon, I said, "It wasn't uneventful." Which was true. The ongoing feud between Lydia Beals and Ashley Krupps had provided endless hours of amusement — for everyone other than the Snob Squad, since we'd all been there. To Mom I said, "It wasn't memorable, either. I forget."

Mom aimed her corn dog at me. "You want your

father and me to communicate more, but whenever we try —"

"Look at the time," Dad interrupted Mom mid-rampage. "We better get going, hon. We don't want the medical meter to start running without us."

She finished her corn dog, dabbed at her mouth with a napkin, and stood.

"Where are you going?" I asked.

"You know," Mom answered. "Marriage counseling."

Dad faked a smile. "If we're not back by morning, go ahead and put yourselves up for adoption."

I laughed. Van didn't. She bit her lip, looking worried.

In the doorway Mom slipped on a sweater and said, "Don't make any plans for Friday night. We're doing something together."

As soon as the back door closed, Van and I exchanged expressions of horror. "God, I hope whatever we do is out of state." I switched her dinner with mine.

Van was quiet as she cut the pear into a dozen identically sized pieces. Stabbing the first piece with one fork tine, she said, "Do you think they'll make it?"

A frown creased my brow. "Make what?"

"You know, make it. Stay together."

Swirling Vanessa's corn dog in Mom's leftover

ketchup, I smiled in anticipated bliss. "They have t
I chomped off the end and finished in a garble, "For
the children."

Vanessa met my eyes and held. "News flash," she
said. "We're not children anymore."

Which made my corn dog go mealy in my mouth.

Chapter 3

I stepped down from the bus on Friday morning to find Prairie and Max waiting for me. "Where's Lydia?" I asked.

"In the temp." Max thumbed over her shoulder.

"We should g-go help her fix her diorama," Prairie said.

Slinging my backpack over one shoulder, I led the way to the trailer. "I tried to call Lydia last night," I told them, "but the phone just rang and rang."

"I tried, too," Prairie said. "She sure was upset yesterday. I've n-never seen Lydia do anything like that."

"Me neither." Lydia Beals had a reputation as the biggest brown-noser in the history of the world.

Max said, "I heard all Krupps had to do was write a letter of apology."

"What?!" My jaw hit the pavement. "No wonder Lydia went ballistic."

We all fumed for her. "Lydia's right," I said. "Ashley gets away with murder. Remember that time *someone* flushed Lydia's gym shorts down the toilet? It overflowed and since no one confessed, we all had to run laps."

"I remember that," Prairie said.

"We all knew who did it." I seethed. "But Ashley puts on this horrified, innocent act. Then she claims she has a sprained ankle and can't run, so we end up getting her punishment."

Max shook her head. "She never got busted for the graffiti in the girl's restroom, either. Everybody knows she did it. Who else dots their *i*'s with little hearts?"

Sometimes I did, but now was not the time to mention that.

"The problem is," Max went on, "no one ever catches Krupps in the act."

"I know," Prairie and I said together. Prairie pointed. "Hey, there's Lydia."

Jogging down the sidewalk from the temps, Lydia stopped in front of us and bent over, wheezing.

"Lyd, you all right?" I put a hand on her back.

"I'm okay." She erected herself. "Just an asthma attack. Probably set off by Melanie's perfume." She stuck out her tongue.

"We were coming to help you fix your diorama," Prairie told her.

"Forget it," Lydia muttered. "*They're* in there." She curled a lip. We all knew who she meant.

"Is it true all Ashley had to do was write you a letter of apology?" I asked.

Behind her glasses, Lydia's eyes narrowed. "Plus, help undo the damage. Like I care anymore." She stared off across the playground, adding, "Someday, somehow, justice will be served."

I hoped she was right, but doubted it.

As we wandered over toward the bleachers, our usual morning hangout, I said to Lydia, "I tried to call you last night, but your phone just kept ringing."

"That's because I unplugged it after Mrs. Jonas called," she replied. "She left a message for my mom, which I erased. Thank God I got to the answering machine first."

"What did your mom say when you told her what happened yesterday?" I asked.

"I didn't tell her."

Prairie, Max, and I exchanged surprised glances. Lydia told her mother everything, or so I thought. Since it was only the two of them, Lydia and her mom had a really close relationship. Even though her mom could be a little overprotective, I sort of envied Lydia's home life.

We sat on the bleachers, Lydia and Max behind

Prairie and me. Prairie asked first. "Why d-didn't you tell her?"

I twisted around to face Lydia. "Yeah, Lydia. Your mom would be down here in a second raising hell with Mr. Krupps."

"I know." She let out a short breath. "But Mom told me last time she was getting a little tired of fighting all my battles. She said I needed to figure out how to deal with people like Ashley; that there'd always be someone in my life trying to take advantage of my good nature."

That was a depressing thought. "Did she give you any tips?" I asked.

"Nothing that would work. All this psychology crap. Like 'Try to find out the reason she's targeting you.' 'Sit down and conduct a dialog.' 'Strike a mutual agreement.' Blah, blah, blah." Lydia rolled her eyes.

"How do you conduct a dialog with sewer sludge?" I muttered.

Lydia blinked at me and howled. She had this really obnoxious hyena howl, but it didn't bother me at the moment. It was good to hear Lydia laughing again.

The warning bell rang and we meandered slowly across the soccer field to the trailers. Surrounded by the Snob Squad, I suddenly felt at home. My friends were like my family — my family of choice as opposed to the ones I got stuck with. Before this year, I hated coming to school. Dreaded every moment. But now, with the Squad (not to mention my daily dose of Kevin Rooney), I dreaded the thought of school ending.

As soon as roll was taken, Mrs. Jonas handed out the weekly reports of our missing assignments. This week she'd listed everything we'd missed over the last grading period. Mine ran on for three pages.

Mrs. Jonas said, "I've cleared it with Mr. Biekmund for you to skip science lab today and Monday, if you need to stay here and work."

My eyes scanned the room and came to a crashing halt on Kevin. He pointed to the floor with his index finger and mimed, "Stay." Which sealed my decision.

Just about everybody stayed. Unfortunately, Mrs. Jonas was serious about working. She wouldn't even let us visit quietly.

Lydia, whose only unfinished assignment had to be her social studies project, immediately removed one of her trashy romance paperbacks from her backpack and immersed herself in it. Rats. Helping her was going to be my excuse to move closer to Kevin.

I actually completed two math practice sheets and a geography map of Africa, whatever continent it's on. But the effort cost me. My foot fell asleep and my stomach was growling like a grizzly for a sugar fix. As I was digging in my desk for an old malted milk ball or something, a knock sounded on the door. Mrs. Jonas rose from her seat and tiptoed over.

"Mrs. Jonas, you have a call from your ex-husband in the office. He says it's an emergency." Needless to say, all ears tuned in. That's the danger of complete silence.

Mrs. Jonas whispered to us, "I'll be right back." Her eyes darted around. "Jenny," she said, "you're in charge."

Oh, great. My reward for being so responsible yesterday. The door hadn't even whooshed shut before everyone transformed into their natural selves — zoo animals. The chimpanzees started hurdling over desks and chasing each other around the room, while the elephants stampeded out the back door. I noticed Hugh take Prairie by the hand and slip behind the big comfy chair next to Mrs. Jonas's desk.

Kevin sauntered over to me, which I hoped meant he had ideas of his own. Which he did. "You want to play hangman at the board?" he asked.

"Sure," I said. Hyperventilating from the thrill, I followed him to the blackboard. There were only nibs of chalk in the tray, so Kevin headed back to Mrs. Jonas's desk to find a new stick. Behind the comfy chair, I heard low murmurs. Whatever they were doing back there, it wasn't daily oral language.

"You go first." Kevin handed me a chalk. As I prepared to draw my gallows, Kevin took my hand, opened it, and filled it with M&M's.

"Kevin." My eyes grew wide. "Are these from Mrs. Jonas's reward jar?"

He grinned. "She won't notice. It was almost empty."

I'd been eyeing that jar all year, drooling as the level of M&M's decreased, no thanks to me.

A paper airplane whizzed by my cheek and Kevin launched it back over my shoulder. It sailed toward the door, where Mrs. Jonas was standing, arms folded. The din took a sudden plunge. Mrs. Jonas's eyes held mine. All she said was, "Thank you, Jenny."

I choked on my M&M's. Talk about feeling like a worm.

When we got back from lunch, there was a surprise waiting for us. Mr. Krupps was standing at the front of the room, scowling. I think he was scowling; it's hard to tell with principals. "Take your seats," he ordered us. His tone of voice confirmed his mood.

Mrs. Jonas hovered behind Mr. Krupps, her arms wrapped loosely around her waist. Mr. Krupps said,

"Mrs. Jonas has just discovered a sizable amount of money missing from her purse."

A gasp of horror sucked up all the air. Wide eyes focused on Mrs. Jonas. Her chin fell to her chest.

"How much?" I asked without thinking.

"That doesn't matter," Mr. Krupps barked at me, making me shrivel. He went on, "The issue is, someone got into Mrs. Jonas's purse."

Mrs. Jonas blinked up. "I don't think it was any of you." Glancing around the room, she added softly, "Was it?"

You could feel eyeballs squirming in their sockets. When no one spoke, Mr. Krupps said, "If anybody knows anything about this, if you saw someone in here when they weren't supposed to be, or heard anyone talking about it, speak up."

I thought the silence was deafening until Mr. Krupps slammed his fist into the nearest desk. "I will *not* tolerate criminal activity here at Montrose. I run a clean school. Safe and secure, for students and teachers. No one leaves this room until we clear this matter up."

Geez, what did he expect? A public confession? Get real.

"Daddy?" Ashley raised a tentative hand.

Oh, figures, I thought. To the list of stuck-up, spoiled, and snotty, we were about to add snitch.

"I don't know if it means anything," she said in a sickly sweet voice, "but a bunch of people were hanging around Mrs. Jonas's desk this morning while she was out taking a phone call. Including Max."

My head whipped around to catch Max's reaction. It was, in a word, nuclear. "I was handing in assignments," Max snarled.

"Hey, I was there," I volunteered. "She didn't do anything —" I stopped short. Of course, I wasn't focusing on anyone's activities besides Kevin's.

"I just thought I'd mention it." Ashley shrugged.

I'll kill her, I thought. If Max doesn't get to her first.

Lydia piped up, "Could it have happened before school?"

Mr. Krupps queried Mrs. Jonas. "It could have," she admitted. "I cashed my check last night, and my purse was in my desk all day."

A slow smile spread across Lydia's lips. "I was in the room before school and Ashley and Melanie were in here, supposedly working on a project."

Ashley twisted in her seat. She was so fat, her desk moved with her. "You were here, too."

"Not as long as you," Lydia shot back.

Melanie said, "Max was here when me and Ashley got here. Remember that, Ash?"

Ashley's beady eyes gleamed. "Now that you mention it, I do."

"I came in to feed the fish," Max growled. "Like I always do."

Always? She never told us that. I knew she got to school before my bus arrived, but I thought it was to check out a basketball before the boys snagged them all.

"Maxine, to the office," Mr. Krupps ordered.

She didn't budge.

"Now!" he bellowed, aiming an index finger at the door.

"Hold on." Mrs. Jonas stepped forward. "Max does have permission to feed . . ." At Mr. Krupps's glare, her voice trailed off.

He said, "Everyone is a suspect until we get this cleared up. Maxine, I'll talk to you first." He wrenched open the door and waited for Max.

She slammed her desk shut and stood. The floor trembled as she stomped past. At the front, she paused at Melanie's desk. Deliberately, she plopped her leg atop it and shoved her foot at Melanie. Melanie impaled herself against the seat slats.

"Get a good look," Max said. "This is your face."

"McFarland!" Mr. Krupps warned.

She flew past him out the door. He had to hustle to

catch up. Mrs. Jonas stared out the windows past them. We all did. My blood boiled. Everyone always assumes Max is guilty.

So why did I feel guilty? Maybe because if the theft occurred during the time I was room monitor, this whole fiasco was my fault.

We stopped in the office after lunch to see Max, figuring she got in-school suspension just for being born, but she wasn't there. Which worried me.

As I was hustling to catch my bus after school, I just caught the tail end of a conversation Ashley and Melanie were having on the front steps. Ashley, who was braiding Melanie's hair, said, "Yeah, and my dad says anyone who carries around a lot of cash deserves to be robbed."

My jaw cracked the stoop. I thought, She did it. Ashley Krupps stole that money. A slow smile creased my lips. Well, well, well. What would her father say when he found out his precious little angel was a thief? No way he could let something that serious slide. Another thought barreled through my brain: Now all we have to do is prove it.

Chapter 4

Dear Dopey Food Diary,

After school I ate three Oreo cookies. If I didn't have to write it down, I would've eaten a whole row. But since I promised to tell you the truth, the whole truth, and nothing but the truth, you'll just have to trust me. I actually controlled myself.

I paused, flicking my Bic in and out. Then I wrote,

Mrs. Jonas got robbed and Max got busted. Max didn't do it — not this time. I know who did, though. When I called Max after school to find out what happened with Mr. Krupps and tell her what I heard, she informed me she got a real suspension. Three whole days.

I asked her how Krupps could suspend her without proof and she didn't answer. Then her brother needed to use the phone so she had to hang up.

I paused. The question lingered. How could he suspend her without proof? Unless . . . no, forget it. Max didn't do it.

Anyway, I don't know why I'm telling you this. What do you care? Unless I eat my words.

"Jenny, shake your booty," Dad hollered down the hall. "We're going to be late."

I closed my food diary and bounded over to the dresser to check for Oreo traces in my teeth. As I trundled to the living room where the family unit was waiting, I asked casually, "Late for what?" Then I remembered: Mom had said not to make plans for tonight. "Where are we going?"

Dad smiled slyly. "It's a surprise." Dad wiggled his eyebrows.

Vanessa rolled her eyes at me. I reciprocated. I hate surprises.

Mom had changed from her work clothes into jeans and a sweatshirt. At least I was dressed for the occasion in my baggy overalls. Whatever the family togetherness activity was, I hoped it wouldn't take long. I didn't want to miss a call from Kevin.

It was just starting to sprinkle as Dad backed our old Subaru station wagon out of the garage. No one spoke the whole time, which wasn't unusual. I don't know about Van, but I was trying to figure out where we were headed. It didn't help that the rain was turning into a monsoon and blurring all the street signs. After about twenty minutes, Dad slowed the car and said, "Surprise! This is it."

"This is what?" I leaned over the seat and squinted ahead. Through the downpour, a neon sign flashed: BO L VA D OW ING.

"No." Vanessa slithered down her seat belt. "I won't go. You can't make me."

Believe it or not, my sister is fifteen.

"Go where?" I said.

Mom twisted around and answered, "Bowling."

I just about lost my cookies. "You're not serious."

"Serious as sauerkraut," Dad said.

Gag. I said what I was thinking: "No one goes bowling anymore," adding to myself, Especially with their parents.

"You wanted to do more things together, so from now on Friday night is family night." Dad yanked up the parking brake.

Mom said, "We'll have to make a run for it. Ready? Go!" She opened her door and shot out.

Stomping through puddles with only our arms to

cover our heads, Vanessa pulled up beside me and snarled, "This is all your fault."

I opened my mouth to argue, then I wondered if she was right. I mean, I wanted our family to be more of a family. I was in favor of making dinnertime our family time. But it wasn't my idea to spend every waking moment together, which seemed to be Mom and Dad's interpretation. We were starting to drive each other nuts. And I'm not talking lightly salted.

Standing, dripping, in the entryway, Mom hollered over the bowling alley racket, "Robert, why don't you go get us a lane and I'll buy something to eat." To us she said, "You two look for balls and shoes."

"If anyone I know sees me here, I'll die," Vanessa muttered as she skulked down the alley. "This is like the ultimate humiliation. It is *so* Neanderthal."

My sister is overly dramatic. Unlike me. "Oh, my God!" I screeched to a stop. "You can't be serious. These shoes are used."

"Duh." Vanessa curled a lip at me. "You act like you've never been bowling before."

"I haven't."

"Yes, you have. We went once when you were like four years old."

"Give me a break," I said. "The only thing I remember from my early years is falling down the stairs and breaking my arm."

Vanessa frowned at me. "That wasn't you. That was me."

"Really? Then I don't remember anything." Which was scary. Maybe I was abducted by aliens. My eyes strayed back to Dad, who was eyeing the bowling lanes, smiling hypnotically. Maybe I'd never returned.

Vanessa pulled out a pair of shoes and sniffed them. Her nose puckered. She dug down deep into her bush bag and said, "Here, use this." She handed me a moist towelette. "I'd advise you to wipe out the finger holes on the bowling balls, too."

Did I mention my sister is also obsessive/compulsive? Her condition has improved — she doesn't zone out as often as she used to — but only an obsessive/compulsive would carry a whole canister of moist towelettes. I wondered what else was in her two-ton canvas bag. A new pair of shoes, perhaps? I could squeeze into a six if I had to.

I spotted Mom first, or maybe my nose did. She was carrying a tray of hamburgers and fries and drinks. No sign of cottage cheese, thank goodness. Maybe this wouldn't be so bad after all. I made a mental note: Dear Fatty Food Diary, know all the dieting I did this week? Blow it off.

We trailed Mom over to our lane. Dad was sitting at the controls, cranking up the scoreboard, which was huge and lit-up. When he wrote down my name, I freaked.

"Dad," I said, wrenching down his writing arm, "everyone can see our scores. Don't use our real names."

He met my eyes and saw that I was serious. "Who do you want to be?" he asked.

I considered the question. "Ashley Krupps," I replied.

He smiled and wrote, *Aslee Craps*.

Close enough. Apparently Vanessa and I got our defective spelling genes from him.

Mom was up first. At the end of the lane, she poised with her ball, aimed, and threw. The ball thudded on the lane, bounced, and rolled down the aisle. Straight toward the middle pin. Which toppled and set up a chain reaction. When the last pin dropped, Mom shrieked and jumped for joy.

Beside me, Vanessa muttered, "I was switched at birth."

"You're up, Van," Dad said.

"Do I have to?"

Mom gave Vanessa the look. You know the one: Life is short, especially yours if you keep this up. Vanessa exhaled in disgust. She rose from her seat, stormed to the machine, grabbed her ball, and flung it. It rolled right into the gutter. She stormed back.

"We'll call that a practice shot," Dad said.

"You can't," Mom told him. "It's automatic scoring. No free balls."

Vanessa grumbled, "Let's call it a night." She threw her second ball, also into the gutter, then slumped over in her seat.

Dad was next. He stood with his ball, gazing down the lane. Then he wiggled his hips, aimed, and threw. He was left with what he called the dreaded seven-ten split, which apparently meant there were two pins still standing, one on each side.

I'm no physics whiz, but even I know you can't hit two pins, a hundred feet apart, with one ball. And Dad missed both pins. Then he said a really bad word.

"Robert!" Mom scolded him. "Really."

I was next. My ball was heavier than I remembered, and the finger holes were smaller. The worst part was waddling up to the line. Everyone who was bowling stopped to gawk. "Go ahead," I said to the bowlers on either side of me. "I'm testing the wind."

They both rolled strikes.

I studied their form. Tried to copy it. But as my arm swung back, my fingers lost their grip. The ball clunked behind me, right after my arm popped out of its socket. Everyone in the universe watched my ball roll off the alley and under a seat. Vanessa covered her mouth. Dad's shoulders shook.

"Shut up." I scowled at them.

Mom said, "Honey, I don't think that's your ball."

Oh, gee. Is that why I blew a disk in my spine?

Dad retrieved the ball and took it back, while I tested the other balls. After picking out the lightest, I tried bowling again. This time my ball found its mark — the gutter.

You know how when you rent a horse to go horseback riding, and all it ever does is head back to the barn? Think of my ball as the horse, and the gutter as the barn. By the fifth frame I had a score of zero. Vanessa got lucky once. Her score was three.

When Mom hit her third strike in five frames, I could feel Dad bristle. Then Vanessa shrieked, "Oh, my God!" She whipped her head around and whispered into my shoulder, "I know him. Don't let him see me."

I peered around her. Three people were coming toward us. Vanessa thought *she* was in trouble. Two of them, *I* knew.

Chapter 5

When our eyes connected, Prairie called, "Hey, Jenny." She waved her free hand. The other hand was held by Hugh. He grinned at me.

Prairie hobbled down to our lane, with Hugh in tow. Thank God Kevin wasn't with them. Kevin and Hugh were sort of friends, but only because they shared an interest in computers (not to mention members of the Snob Squad).

I don't know why I was shocked to see Prairie and Hugh. I knew Hugh's favorite sport was bowling. Before the spring fling, when Prairie told us she liked Hugh Torkerson and we decided it was our duty to get Hugh to ask her to the dance, Lydia had concocted this phony survey — a questionnaire to find out a bunch of stuff about Hugh so that we could devise a plan. One of the questions was, "What is your favorite sport?" And Hugh had answered, "Bowling."

Basketball is a sport. Baseball is a sport. Even badminton is a sport, sort of. But bowling? There was a reason Hugh was known as Tork the Dork.

"I didn't know you liked to b-bowl," Prairie said to me.

I saw Hugh studying the scoreboard. "It's my first time," I said quickly.

"Mine, too." Prairie smiled demurely. "Hugh's going to teach me." She beamed up at him.

I couldn't take my eyes off their intertwined fingers. The closest Kevin's hand had come to mine was the M&M's exchange. It made me wonder if Prairie had ordered her wedding cake.

"Hugh and his cousin Bruce are on a team," Prairie added.

"In a bowling league," Bruce said, stepping out from behind Hugh.

Pummel me with a nine pin. Bruce was probably Vanessa's age. He must've been the one she recognized. Bruce was also as far from a nerd as any guy could get. Jet black hair with sky blue eyes, his huge muscles bulged out of his cutoff denim shirt. Hugh still had his pocket protector in.

"Notice anything different about me?" Prairie said.

I scanned her. She looked radiant. The way she always did around Hugh. Without thinking, I blurted, "You grew a foot?"

Prairie looked stunned.

Oh, man. Talk about insensitive. Prairie wears a prosthesis because she was born with a deformed foot. "I, I meant —"

She cut me off with a giggle. "Jenny," she said as she kicked my bowling shoe with her prosthesis. She said, "No, silly. Here." She brushed back the hair over her left ear. In the fluorescent light, something sparkled.

"Prairie!" I jumped up. My hand automatically reached over to touch her earring. It was a half moon; the other half was on the other ear. "Is it — are they — real gold?"

"Fourteen karat," Hugh said as he puffed out his pocket protector.

"Hugh gave them to me," Prairie said.

"Well, I didn't think Bugs Bunny did."

Prairie laughed. Hugh didn't get it. "Karats?" I repeated. "Bunny?"

"Oh," he snorkled.

What, I wondered for the trillionth time, did she see in him?

Prairie said, "It's an anniversary present."

Anniversary? They'd only been together since the dance.

As if reading my mind, Prairie added, "Our one-week anniversary."

Wow, if she got gold after a week, what would she get for the entire month of May?

I was in awe. I was jealous. Kevin hadn't gotten up to gift giving, and I didn't know if he ever would.

"Ashley, your turn," Dad said.

Still staring at Prairie's earrings, I said, "You take it, Dad. You need the practice."

Wrong thing to say. Mom laughed.

"Is Ashley here?" Prairie peered around me.

"No," I said, then freaked. "I hope not." My eyes scanned the bowling alley to be sure. The whole school would know my score by Monday with her gutter mouth. "I'm Ashley," I told Prairie and Hugh. "I'm not, really. It's just for tonight."

They both looked vacant.

"Never mind."

From the scoring station, Mom called, "You're leading with your wrong foot, Robert. That's your problem."

Dad's spine went rigid. He threw the ball and it bounced. Right into the gutter.

Mom said, "Try starting over to the right a little. Use the lane arrows."

Dad turned and smiled. It wasn't a friendly "Gosh, honey, thanks for the advice" smile, either. Under his breath, he snarled, "I'll lead with any damn foot I want."

Storming back to the table, he spilled his beer and cursed real loud.

I cringed. Vanessa dug her head deeper into her bush bag.

"She's right, you know," Hugh said. "He should lead with his left."

Prairie must've sensed my father's imminent implosion because she yanked Hugh away. "We b-better get going," she said. "Bruce is getting impatient."

Bruce was getting a date. He stood behind a girl on the next lane over, showing her how to swing the ball. Maybe if Mom used that approach on Dad. . . .

Crraack! Mom rolled another strike. She started to shriek, then saw the look on Dad's face and shrugged.

It was a fabulously fun family night. Fortunately no one captured it on film for the Solano Moments to Remember family album. Which we'd start someday.

Chapter 6

Not only was family night a bust, it made me miss Kevin's phone call. There were three messages on the machine. Two hang-ups, which had to be Kevin because I'd know his hang-ups anywhere, and Lydia. "Jenny, call me immediately!" She sounded desperate. So what else is new? "Don't call after nine, though. My mom doesn't allow me to talk on the phone after nine."

She only told me this every other day. I checked my watch. Nine-twenty. Great. Guess I'd have to wait till morning to see what the emergency was.

I tried calling Lydia the next morning. No answer. All weekend I kept trying. It made me mad because I never heard from Kevin either. I figured he was trying to call me while I was dialing Lydia. Which I could've confirmed if Dad didn't believe call waiting was too rude to use. Whatever. Lydia was ruining my love life.

That's what dieting does to me. Makes me irritable

and irrational. No doubt I missed Kevin's calls because Vanessa was constantly gabbing on the phone with her new friend, Phoebe the flautist.

"I need my own phone," I informed Mom and Dad at dinner. "I'm missing all my important calls." In a moment of brilliance, I added, "And you're missing yours, because I'm tying up the only phone in the house."

"That's the truth," Vanessa said.

I couldn't decide if I should sneer or thank her for her support.

In unison, Mom and Dad glanced up and barked, "No!"

It made me back off quick. They were still steamed about family fun night. Good thing they had marriage counseling on Monday. Van met my eyes. She was obviously wondering the same thing I was: Would they stay married till then?

As soon as I stepped off the bus Monday morning, Lydia attacked me. "I talked to Max on Saturday and she sounded really depressed. I think we should meet at the Peacemobile and see what's going on with her."

The Peacemobile was our secret meeting place. It was an old rusted-out VW minivan that belonged to Max's brother, Scuzz-Gut. The van was parked in his used auto parts establishment behind their house.

"Did she say if she took the money?"

"Jenny!" Lydia slapped my arm. "I didn't ask her."

"Scared of the answer, huh?"

Lydia smirked.

"I'm just kidding. We all know who did it," I said.

"We do?" Through her glasses, Lydia's eyes magnified.

"Of course. Ashley." I repeated the conversation I'd overheard on Friday.

Lydia shook her head. "That sounds like the kind of asinine remark she'd make."

"You mean it sounds like the kind of incriminating remark she'd make. No way Mr. Krupps could blow off something like this. I mean, stealing from a teacher? That's got to be a felony or something. Remind me to ask Max."

Lydia giggled and slapped me again.

"If only we could prove Ashley did it," I said.

Lydia nodded slowly. "If only." As we walked past the bike racks, she turned to me. "I found out how much was stolen. Eighty-five dollars."

My eyes bulged. "Geez."

"That's what I wanted to talk to you about. Well, one of the things."

"I tried to call you all weekend," I told her. "Where were you?"

Lydia replied, "My mom had to give this talk at some church retreat and she was leaving Saturday night. She said I couldn't come so I had to stay with my day care provider."

Your baby-sitter, you mean. I didn't say it.

"I wanted to stay with you instead."

"You could have. I didn't do anything all weekend." Besides make the *Guinness Book of World Records* for lowest bowling score ever and camp out by the phone waiting for Kevin to call.

"Can we meet after school today?" Lydia asked.

"Fine by me," I said. "Where's Prairie?"

"With Hugh, of course. Over by the bleachers. Probably making out."

"No way."

"You saw what he got her for their anniversary, didn't you?" Lydia rolled her eyes.

Okay, way. But I didn't say it; didn't even want to think it.

Kevin materialized from under the stands and Lydia said in a sing-song, "Here comes *your* lover boy. Kiss kiss."

"Shut up." I elbowed her hard enough to break a rib.

"Hey, Jen," Kevin said.

"Hey," I said back casually, even though my heart was hammering hip-hop.

"Hi, Kevie," Lydia said. "Whatcha got?"

He stopped in front of us, hiding something behind his back. His eyes held on Lydia, like she had a festering scab on her nose. "Could I see you for a minute?" He blinked over to me.

"Take a hint, Lyd," I said, not taking my eyes off Kevin.

Beside me, Lydia bristled. "I just remembered something I have to do. Something more important than being with my best friend."

"Better go, then," I said.

In a huff, Lydia stormed off.

Feeling guilty, I called, "See you later, Lyd. In like two minutes."

Kevin murmured, "I thought she'd never leave."

I laughed. Okay, it wasn't that funny, but his nearness was making me giddy.

"I called you Friday night, but no one was home," he said. "And I had baseball camp all weekend."

See? I know his buzz on the machine. "Yeah, we had this family thing on Friday." I made a face. After we got married, I'd fill him in on my family. No sense jeopardizing the union at this stage.

"Drag." He scraped a foot across the gravel. Without warning, he whipped his hand out from behind his back and handed me a box. It was a little square white box covered in comics newspaper, then taped all over. "I'm not too good a wrapper," he said.

He was so adorable. Patient, too. The box was wrapped tight as a Tootsie Roll. It took me about ten minutes to dig off one little strip. Finally Kevin drew out a Swiss Army knife from his front jeans pocket and slit the bottom. Since knives were highly illegal at school, he quickly hid it.

I opened the box and gasped. Inside was a pair of earrings. Like Prairie's, except mine were gold hearts. "Oh, my God!" I blinked up at him. "Are these for me?"

"No, they're for Lydia. Could you give them to her?"

I whapped his arm.

He asked, "You want me to help you put them on?"

Goosebumps prickled my whole body. The thought of him touching me . . . "Uh, sure." I shivered.

While Kevin fiddled with a clasp on one of the posts, I removed my other earrings. They were fake pearls that I bought at Dollar Daze when I was eight. "I went with Hugh to pick out earrings for Prairie, and I didn't want you to be jealous," Kevin said.

He didn't want me to be jealous? How sweet.

Kevin squinted as he took aim at my ear. His fin-

gers on my earlobe made it tingle. He poked me and
frowned. "Sorry," he said, stepping back. "This
makes me kind of nervous."

"That's okay. I can put them on easier myself." Ex-
pertly I felt around and stuck the posts through my
holes. "Be thankful it's not my nose that's pierced."

He laughed.

The bell rang. We hustled toward the trailer.
Halfway there, we met up with Prairie and Hugh.
Prairie noticed first. "Jenny, you got . . ."

I brushed my hair aside. "Just like yours."

"Neato," Hugh said.

I looked at Prairie. She was gazing up at Hugh as if
she was witnessing the reincarnation of Hercules.
Love is blind. Apparently deaf and dumb, too.

Hugh said to Kevin, "Did you tell Jenny we got a
great deal? Fifty dollars a pair, or two for seventy-
nine dollars and ninety-nine cents. Plus tax."

"Hugh!" Kevin shoved him. He shook his head at
Hugh, like he was a hopeless case, which he was.

But my eyes popped out of their sockets. Seventy-
nine dollars and ninety-nine cents? Where would
Kevin and Hugh get . . . my stomach lurched. No
way. I fought the thought. Forget it. Not Kevin. Not
ever, never, never.

Chapter 7

We settled into our places in the Peacemobile — Lydia, Prairie, and me on the saggy flowered sofa, and Max in her beanbag chair. As I passed around a bag of Orville Redenbacher's popcorn cakes, I thought, Something's different about Max. Out of place.

"These things taste like Styrofoam," Lydia said, sticking out her tongue.

"They have to," I replied. "They're diet food. You're not supposed to enjoy them." I crunched into a cake, wishing I had a case of Coke to wash it down.

Max crossed one foot over her knee, and that's when it struck me. "Max, you got your shoes!"

She shrugged one shoulder and smiled. The sneakers were so big and white that when they caught the light they nearly blinded me.

"Nice," Lydia said, examining them up close. "How much did they cost?"

"None of your beeswax." Max dropped her foot. She snatched the bag of popcorn cakes out of Lydia's hand.

I knew how much leather sneakers like that cost — a hundred dollars, easy.

Max mumbled, "I got 'em on sale."

It was quiet suddenly, all of us avoiding eye contact. Could they be wondering what I was? "So, uh, Max," I asked tentatively, "how come you got suspended?"

If she said it was because she stole the money, I'd spit my popcorn cake across the van.

Max snapped off an edge of cake and chewed. We all waited. Finally, she answered, "I might've called Krupps a couple of names." Her eyes narrowed. "But he deserved it. He didn't even bother to ask if I took the money; just assumed I was guilty." Her jaw clenched. Taking another bite, she chewed and swallowed before meeting our eyes and asking, "You don't think I did it, do you?"

"No, no, of course not," we all said together. "No way."

She added, "I don't even know how much was taken."

"Eighty-five dollars," I informed her.

Prairie gasped. Max blinked at me. "How do you know?"

"I, uh, Lydia told me."

All eyes zoomed in on Lydia. "I heard Ashley tell Melanie," she said quickly. "Tell them what else Ashley said, Jenny."

I repeated Ashley's comment about people who carry around too much cash deserving to be robbed. Max growled, "That's cold, man." We nodded agreement.

The bag of popcorn cakes made the rounds. "Eighty-five dollars," Prairie repeated. "That's a l-lot of money."

"Yeah, like my whole summer allowance." I sighed. Thinking aloud, I said, "I wish I had eighty-five dollars. I could use a whole new summer wardrobe. Like I'll ever be thin enough to wear shorts."

"Oh, Jenny, you look fine," Lydia lied.

"Yeah, right."

"K-Kevin thinks so," Prairie said.

My face flared. He'd never seen my flabby thighs, and he never would.

Prairie added, "I know what I'd do with eighty-five dollars." She picked off a piece of popcorn from her cake and nibbled on it.

We waited. Finally Lydia exhaled impatiently. "Well, what, Prairie? What would you do?"

Prairie popped the kernel into her mouth, chewed, and swallowed. "I'd g-give it to poor people."

Lydia curled a lip. "Like who?"

"Ashley Krupps," I answered. "She's a poor excuse for a person."

Lydia hyena howled. After she recovered, she said, "Really, Prairie, like what poor people?"

Prairie's eyes dropped. "Like Hugh."

"Hugh's poor?" I gaped at her. It was a sobering thought. He did look poor, come to think of it. Not that I knew what poor looked like. Everyone looked a little grungy at the end of a school year, but who could blame us? We'd just survived nine months of incarceration.

Even though Hugh's shirts were a little shabby, he still dressed nicer than most of the guys. If he wasn't Kevin's friend, I might call him a Eugene. Maybe I did.

Prairie said, "His dad's on d-disability. And his mom just got laid off."

"So where'd he get the money to buy you gold earrings?" Lydia asked.

Prairie blushed as she felt her left earlobe. In a small voice she said, "I don't know. Maybe he found it."

Lydia snorted.

I didn't say what I was thinking. Because I didn't want to be thinking it about Hugh or Kevin. I noticed Max was awfully quiet, sitting there in her gleaming new Air Zooms. No, I chided myself, don't go there. Max didn't do it. "Look, we all know Ashley stole Mrs. Jonas's money. But here we are again without any proof."

Lydia said, "What about what she said to Melanie?"

"It's incriminating, yeah. But it's not proof."

Lydia blinked at me. "Well, she knew how much was taken. Isn't that proof?"

I shook my head. "She'll just lie and say someone told her. I mean, everyone has to know by now how much was stolen. No, the only way to prove it would be to catch her with the money. Unfortunately, anyone with half a brain would've already spent it." I paused. "Which means she probably still has it."

Prairie giggled and nudged me with her fake foot.

A plan was coming together in my head. "I bet if we looked in her purse we'd find the money."

We all exchanged glances. Lydia's eyes lit up.

"Hey, don't do anything till I get back," Max said. "I want to be in on the kill."

A current of warmth spread around the group. Automatically, we did the Snob Squad salute: finger to nose to Ashley.

Chapter 8

During dinner Mom and Dad informed Vanessa and me that we were going with them to marriage counseling that night.

"Why?" I asked. "We're not married."

Mom just looked at me. I didn't say what I was thinking: Neither will *you* be at this rate. I can't believe they were still angry about family fun night. Geesh. Get over it. Their anger hung in the air like smog.

"Not that I won't ever be married," I added quickly. "Miracles do happen."

Dad swigged his milk and said, "Are you still dating that boy you went to the dance with? Old what's-his-name?"

"His name's Kevin and he's not old." My face fried. "We're not exactly dating." Okay, we were. But the way Dad said it sounded so . . . dated.

Dad added, "Is he the one who calls you every

night and talks for an hour so we keep missing the callback from *Who Wants to Be a Millionaire?*"

Mom must've pinched Dad under the table, because he yelped. That made Mom giggle and Dad smile. Well, good. If nothing else their mutual enjoyment of humiliating me would keep them together.

For about ten minutes.

The spark between them extinguished the moment we piled into the car. There was no gas and Mom got peeved at Dad for not keeping the tank full. Then when we reached the interstate, they had to quibble about what route to take downtown because of the construction, etc., etc. Van and I sighed in unison as we stared out opposite windows.

Mom and Dad's marriage counselor was Dr. Sidwa, my old counselor. Dr. Sid wasn't old, really. Just familiar. I'd gone to him when my mother thought that I was mentally ill because I was fat. He'd pretty much told her my mental illness had nothing to do with my weight. Or something like that. Anyway, Dr. Sid started counseling my parents right away. What does that tell you about who needs a shrink?

As the downtown skyscrapers loomed on the horizon, my eyes strayed to Mom and Dad in the front seat, sitting stiffly, staring straight ahead. Mom still had on her work clothes. She was a suit. You know, corporate executive, professional type? I had no idea what an executive did for a living. Execute? Who? Even after she took Van and me with her on Take Our Daughters to Work Day, we came away mystified. Mostly Mom sat in meetings. Mostly we sat in the break room with a bunch of other daughters, scarfing down donuts.

Dad, on the other hand, was an apron. He did the dishes, cleaned house, shopped. His favorite job in the world was doing laundry. If I had to rate my parents in order of their work value to the world, I'd say Dad one, Mom two.

"You missed the turn," Mom sniped at Dad.

"No, I didn't," Dad sniped back.

Mom let out a long breath, like, Okay, if you say so, nincompoop.

A stab of sadness pierced my heart. It was hard watching my parents have to work at being happy together. Maybe their problem wasn't them. Maybe it was us. I mean, we are problem children. Vanessa's problems seemed to be getting better. Unlike mine. Even if my pounds were melting off, you'd need a magnifying glass to notice. At least I didn't have as much excess baggage as Ashley Krupps. No way. But I could have, if I let myself go. And keeping control was a constant struggle.

My food diary helped. Until I got to the part where

I had to write down how I was feeling. Because I was always feeling hungry.

"Hey, there's a McDonald's." I pointed out the golden arches. "Could we stop for a Big Mac?"

Mom twisted around and frowned at me.

"Well, I had to rush through dinner so I could write down that broccoli-and-tuna casserole crud in my food diary before we left."

Mom didn't reply, just twisted back around.

Dad said, "Maybe we can stop for dessert afterward. We don't want to keep the good doctor waiting, since he charges by the minute."

Mom opened her mouth to retort, but quickly closed it again. Thank God. If we had to hear one more time about how she's the one who paid for their counseling through her group insurance, which she reminded Dad of every time we went, I might have had to roll down the window and scream, "Help! Road rage!"

Dr. Sid welcomed us with his usual, "Ah, the Solanos. My favorite family. Please, zeet, zeet, zeet."

He was weird, but cool. "How is everyone?" He motioned us to the chairs. The best ones were under the air vent, since his office was claustrophobic as a closet. "Tell me about the balling," he said, circling his desk.

We all stopped and stared at him, dumbfounded. Even more than usual.

"The what?" Mom finally said.

"The balling. Your family togetherness activity. When I talked to Robert about having the whole family come tonight, he told me you went balling." Dr. Sid swung his right arm back and forth.

"Bowling," Mom said. "Oh, it was . . . fun." She faked a smile and spread it around thick.

"It was boring," Vanessa said. "And stupid."

That was the truth. Vanessa doesn't mince words, even though sometimes I wish she would.

Mom and Dad looked mortified.

"It wasn't that bad," I lied.

Dr. Sid sat. "Why was it boring?" He leaned forward over his desk blotter, toward Vanessa.

She shrugged.

He looked at me.

Why do I always have to answer the tough questions? "We mostly threw gutter balls. I swear, the gutters are wider than the lanes. Probably saves on Mop and Glow, huh, Dad?"

He smiled a little.

That encouraged me. "Plus, Mom and Dad got into a big fight because Mom's a better bowler than Dad."

"Jenny!" Mom gasped.

Dad glowered at me.

So much for controlling my mouth. In a tiny voice, I added, "Well, it's true. Isn't it?"

"Is this true?" Dr. Sid's bushy eyebrows arched.

Dad folded his hands between his knees and hung his head. "It was my fault. I'm too competitive."

Mom said, "No, it was my fault. I'm the one who's competitive. I know you hate it when anyone gives you advice."

"No, I don't," Dad said to her.

"Yes, you do."

"All right," Dr. Sid cut them off. "It doesn't matter. Does it? I mean, is it something to get so angry about?"

Mom and Dad both burned eye holes in the Oriental rug. "No," they mumbled together.

"So," Dr. Sid said, sounding hopeful again, "have you planned another family togetherness activity for this weekend?"

Vanessa said what I was thinking. "Do we have to?"

Dr. Sid cocked his head at her. "What are you saying, Vanessa?"

When she incinerated in her seat, I piped up. "I think what she means is, we don't have very much fun together. As a family."

"Jenny." Mom sounded hurt. "How can you say that?"

"I don't mean we *can't*," I added quickly. "I mean,

we can. We do. We have." I sagged in surrender. "I think we're trying too hard, you know? To be the perfect family."

Dr. Sid met my eyes. He smiled. Shifting his gaze, he said, "Is that what you meant, Vanessa?"

She flinched. "I guess."

"Robert?"

"Huh?" Dad woke up.

"How do you feel about what Jenny said?"

"Good." He raked his fingers through his hair. "I don't want to stop trying, though. I think we just haven't found an activity we all enjoy."

"Excellent!" Dr. Sid clapped his hands together. "I think you hit the button on the nose."

Dad sucked in a smile. So did I.

Mom said, "We have our own interests, that's all. We're individuals. We raised our girls that way, to be independent thinkers. You can't expect us to like all the same things."

"Of course not." Dr. Sid looked serious. "So, Katherine, do you want to continue your family togetherness activities? I thought it was a wonderful idea, but if you think it's tearing you apart rather than bringing you together . . ." He frowned at Mom.

The room suffocated in silence. After a long moment, Mom said, "I'd like to continue. I enjoy all of us being together, no matter what we're doing."

Dad looked at Mom. He reached over and took her hand.

That made me happy. I snapped my fingers and said, "I know. Let's go skydiving."

Dad choked.

Vanessa smirked. "Or bungee jumping."

"Crocodile hunting," I said. "No, wait. Let's climb Mount Everest. Better yet, they have these mules you can ride down the Grand Canyon. Most people come back alive — I think."

Dad chuckled. "How about something closer to home? And tamer. Fishing. Or camping, maybe."

"Camping. Yeah," I said.

Mom made a face. She sighed and said, "Whatever you decide."

That made me mad. She hated camping. Last time we went, she complained the whole weekend. We didn't have any fun at all. "Why don't you decide?" I said to her.

"Me?" Her face flushed.

Everyone waited.

"All right," she said. "Let's go to a movie."

Perfect, I thought. We can sit in a dark theater and not have to look at each other. Or talk, or interact at all.

"That sounds fine," Dad said. "We haven't been to a movie together in ages. There's that new DeNiro movie I've been wanting to see. Something about the mob and —"

The three of us groaned.

"What?" Dad said.

We didn't even have to answer.

"All right, then you decide," he said to us.

Mom said, "Why don't we let the girls decide?"

Vanessa's and my eyes locked. At the same time we said, "*Bloody Tuesday: The Amputation.*"

Mom and Dad groaned. "No horror. That stuff gives me nightmares. We'll decide later," Dad said. "I'm sure there's something we can all agree on."

That's when I remembered the reason we never went to movies together: We never could agree.

Chapter 9

Dear Family Fun and Fake Food Diary,

Mom started breakfast off with a bang. "So, Jenny," she said. "What are you thinking about?" Which made me choke on my Cheerios. I always do anyway, they're dry as dust, but no way was I going to tell her what was on my mind. Which was mostly Kevin. I could have told them about the theft, but that might've brought the conversation back around to Kevin. So, while I chewed Cheerios and said to Mom, "Let me think," Dad chimed in with his urgent updates. Like how the cost of rib roast rose two bucks, and how he couldn't find the AAA vacuum cleaner bags at Wal-Mart, and how Uncle Ralph was back in town. Which set Mom off because she hates Uncle Ralph. Which made Dad mad because Uncle Ralph is his only brother and family is family, etc., etc.

I stopped writing, sighed, and flipped to the next page.

How did that make me feel? Hungry. So on the way out I snitched a Pop Tart from the pantry. But it was tasteless, too, so I only ate one bite and put it back. Proof that dieting makes me delirious.

Needless to say, I was looking forward to school. As soon as the second bell sounded, though, I knew this day was going to be the remake of *Bloody Tuesday: The Amputation*. Kevin was absent. Horrors! How would I make it through the day without our stolen glances? Without imagining my fingers running through his thick, curly hair? Without planning our wedding and naming our children . . . ?

The whole day was a dud. Max's suspension was as demoralizing as Kevin's absence. Prairie, Lydia, and I couldn't seem to find anything to talk about. It made me antsy for the day to end so I could go home and wait for Kevin to call.

He never did.

That night, while lying in bed staring up at the ceiling, I figured Kevin Rooney either 1) died, 2) moved, or 3) decided to dump me and this was his subtle way of saying, "I can't stand the sight of you, Jenny Solano. What was I thinking, you hideous hippopotamus?"

My life was over.

The next day Kevin was back, but looking so green I thought he might puke if I got close enough to say hello. He was coughing his guts out. We couldn't even hear the homework review over Kevin's hacking, so Mrs. Jonas ordered him to the nurse's office. His empty desk left me feeling empty inside.

Max's desk behind me gave off vacancy vibes, too. All the vibes were weird, as if everyone was avoiding talking about the money. Which is why I noticed Ashley's new purse. It was large and leather and attached to her like a limb. It obviously contained something extremely valuable, such as stolen goods. She took it everywhere, too — to science lab, to the restroom, to recess. Even if she got up to sharpen her glitter pencil, she slipped the shoulder strap across her chest and hugged the purse all the way there and back. I wasn't the only one who noticed.

"She sure has s-something in there she doesn't want anyone to see," Prairie said at lunch as she wound a strand of soggy spaghetti onto her fork.

"Which sure makes me want to see it," I said, crunching a celery stick.

"We might as well forget trying to find the money on her," Lydia said. "I bet she takes that purse in the shower with her."

"You're assuming she showers," I said.

Lydia snorted.

I added, "Did you also notice she and Melanie have on the same outfit? *New* outfits? I wonder how much those cost."

"Yeah," Lydia said. "And Ashley's skirt is about two sizes too small. It keeps riding up. You can almost see her blubberbutt every time she waddles by."

Prairie giggled. I didn't. The word *blubberbutt* makes me wither. I smoothed my own skirt over my knees.

"Maybe when Max gets back she can figure out a way to get hold of Ashley's purse," I said.

At the mention of Max, we all sighed. Prairie asked, "What time is it, Jenny?"

I checked my watch. "Twelve fifty-six."

She dabbed at her mouth and scootched out the end of the bench. "I've got to go," she said, standing.

"Heavy date?" I asked.

Prairie blushed. Which answered the question. "Ms. Milner brought in her new snake. Hugh wanted to see it, so I told him to meet me in the lab. You g-guys want to come, too?"

"Yes," I said.

"No," Lydia said at the same time.

We both looked at her. "I hate snakes." Her whole body shuddered.

So did mine, but I didn't have anything else to do, like stare spellbound at Kevin across the cafeteria.

"Come on, Lydia," I said. "You don't have to touch it or anything."

She pursed her lips. "Oh, all right." After shoving her half-eaten tuna salad sandwich back into her lunch bag, she Velcroed the top shut and slid out.

We followed Prairie to the PC lab, where she spent several hours each day with the other special students. On the way we passed Ashley and Melanie hanging posters in the A wing for the monthly PTA bake sale. "I heard your mommy's running for PTA president," Ashley said to Lydia. "If she wins, instead of a spring fling, we'll probably have diorama days."

Melanie howled.

Before Lydia could bust Ashley's braces, I grabbed her sleeve and yanked her past them. Of course, Lydia had to respond. Over her shoulder, she called, "If you were any fatter, we'd have to have two passing periods. One for you and one for everyone else in school."

Ashley's face turned purple. I shoved Lydia into the PC lab to save her life. As I stood guard to make sure Ashley wasn't going to retaliate, a familiar sound in the lab caught my attention. Kevin's coughing.

I whipped around. Kevin smiled. He was standing beside Hugh at a huge fish tank. My celery melted into mush in my stomach.

Beside me, Prairie asked, "Where's Ms. Milner?"

"Don't know," Hugh said. "The door was un-locked, so we just came in. This is a very fine corn snake. An excellent specimen."

"Yeah, it's cool," Kevin said in a nasally voice.

Prairie went on. "We're not supposed to be here when Ms. Milner's out of the r-room."

"Oh, okay," Hugh said. He backed toward the door.

"We're not doing anything wrong," Kevin coun-tered. He unlatched the screen on the top of the fish tank. "Think it'd be okay if I picked it up?"

Prairie peered back at the open door. "I don't know —"

"Sure it would," I answered for her. "Why not?"

When Kevin lifted the snake out of the aquarium, Lydia shrieked. It made us all freak. Lydia covered her eyes and whirled around. "Keep that thing away from me."

Kevin's eyes twinkled mischievously. He thrust the snake at Lydia. She screamed again. Kevin smirked. He is adorable, but I'm glad he didn't do that to me.

Lydia scurried over to the corner, near Ms. Milner's desk, and hid behind the filing cabinets. After I felt the snake and faked fascination, Kevin and Hugh started talking snake specifics, such as how long a corn snake gets, and how many live mice it eats in a month. That made my lunch turn over again, so I wandered around the room.

Ms. Milner's lab was awesome. There were lots of posters and magazines and books on tape. I envied Prairie her "special-needs student" status. Not that I wanted to be learning disabled (which I doubted Prairie was), but it would be nice to get away from the likes of Ashley Krupps and Melanie Mason for a few hours every day.

Ms. Milner rushed into the room. "Hi, kids," she said. "What are you doing in here?"

We all froze. "We're just l-looking at the corn snake," Prairie replied.

Ms. Milner smiled. "He is beautiful, isn't he?"

"Very," Hugh said.

The first bell rang and Ms. Milner headed over to her desk. She passed me and Lydia on the way and smiled hello. Any other teacher would've written us up for loitering.

"You'd better get back to class," she told us. "But you can come by after school if you want. I'll be here for an hour or so." She dumped a stack of folders on her desk.

"Okay," Hugh said. Even through his greasy glasses, you could see his eyes light up.

On the way back to class, Lydia and I had to make a quick pit stop. A couple of minutes later when we opened the restroom door, we almost collided with a body. Not just any body. Max's body.

"Max!" Lydia cried. "What are you doing —"

Max cut Lydia off with a stranglehold to her neck, wedging her against the wall. "Shut up," she said. "If I get caught on school grounds . . ." She released Lydia and took off toward the exit. Out the door window, I saw Ashley and Melanie pausing to talk with Mr. Krupps in the parking lot. Max was on a direct collision course with them.

"Max!" I hollered to her. She glanced back and I pointed out the window. Looking panicked, she quickly ducked into the PC lab.

"What is she doing here? What is she doing here?" Talk about panicked — Lydia was flapping her hands and wheezing.

"Calm down." I grabbed her wrists. "Max can take care of herself." I hoped.

Chapter 10

We didn't beat the late bell back to homeroom from the PC lab. As we charged around the corner at the end of the hall, Kevin pushed off the wall and sidled up beside us. "Hey, Jen." He coughed and covered his mouth. "Are you going to be home tonight? I thought I'd come by." In a husky voice, he added, "I want to give you something."

"What? Your cold?"

He smirked and nudged my shoulder. It sent a tingle all the way to my toes. "Something better," he said.

"Yo, Rooney," someone called from the doorway of the gym. A bunch of seventh graders, I think. They wiggled their hips and made smoochy sounds. One of them sang, "Rooney's got a girlfriend." And I thought Lydia was immature.

"Jerks," Kevin muttered. He coughed again. "Excuse me while I go infect them." He sprinted off toward the gym.

Lydia said, "What do you think he wants to give you? More jewelry?"

How did I know? I was loopy with love.

At two-thirty Mrs. Jonas gave us free time for the remainder of the day. It was like we'd been let out of Leavenworth, wherever that is. Just as Lydia and I were rushing over to claim the quiet corner so we could play tapes on high volume, a sickly sweet smell permeated the air. If you had a nose, you knew that smell. Old Spice.

Mr. Krupps boomed, "Attention!"

Thirty bodies froze in time.

"What are you, a bunch of hooligans? Everyone sit."

The brown-nosers like Lydia scrambled for their desks. The rest of us sank in place.

"Mrs. Jonas, what's going on here?" Mr. Krupps demanded.

She rose from her desk. "The class earned a half hour of free time," she said. "For good behavior."

Good behavior? That was news to me. That'd be news to the *National Enquirer*.

She added, "We were just getting settled." She glared at Ashley, who had exited the bathroom and was taking her sweet time getting back to her desk. She knocked her books on the floor as she tried to squeeze into her seat, which is impossible with a purse attached to your chest.

In fact, as she tried to adjust the purse sideways, the strap broke. The bag thudded to the floor. It was so overstuffed that something squirted out the top. That something was her billfold, and as it slid across the floor the end flaps unfolded. A whole wad of money was exposed.

Ashley quickly snatched it up.

Since Lydia sat in front of Ashley, she couldn't see the billfold. But Prairie and I could. We looked at each other and dropped our jaws.

Mr. Krupps said, "We've had another theft. I don't know what's going on, or who's doing this, but I expect anyone with information to come forward. I will *not* tolerate this sort of criminal activity in my school. Do you understand?" The blood vessels in Mr. Krupps's forehead throbbed.

Melanie raised her hand. "Who got robbed?" she asked.

Mr. Krupps shot her full of eye daggers. Thank God I hadn't asked. In a gravelly voice, he said, "Ms. Milner in the resource room."

There was a group gasp.

I looked at Prairie. She'd clapped her hand over her mouth. Hugh was watching Prairie, too. At the ready, I guess, in case she fainted. Then, for some reason, Hugh and I both looked at Kevin. He stared straight ahead, expressionless.

The bell rang. Usually the final bell signaled the hysteria to begin. Today we quietly gathered our things and slithered out.

Prairie and Lydia accompanied me to the bus stop. As we passed the A wing, Prairie said, "At least they c-can't blame Max. She wasn't even here."

Lydia and I exchanged glances. Our eyes hit the dirt. Ever wish you hadn't seen something? That you didn't know the truth? Because once you know the truth, you can never unknow it.

Dear Faith in Friends, Frozen Food Diary,
   I can't believe Max did it. I don't believe it. By the way, I ate a Healthy Choice frozen dinner tonight and about puked.

Maybe I should have. It might've calmed my stomach. It wasn't just the plastic pork riblets that made me sick. I couldn't stop visualizing Max rushing into the PC lab. Oh, man. Oh, Max.

The front doorbell interrupted my thoughts, thank goodness. I jumped into action. Not that I was anxious about Kevin's imminent arrival, but I tossed my food diary on the bed and hauled butt down the hall.

Dad was closing the door as I screeched to a stop. "Bible thumpers," he muttered, handing me a religious leaflet. The phone rang in the kitchen.

Vanessa called, "It's for you, Jenny."

I hurried to the kitchen. Shoving the leaflet at Van, I grabbed the phone. "Hello?"

"Hi. It's me."

My shoulders sagged. Not that I didn't want to talk to Prairie.

"M-Max ran away from home," Prairie whispered urgently.

"What? Where?" I said. "When?"

"Today," Prairie answered.

Today? Like right after she robbed Ms. Milner? I couldn't believe I was thinking that. "How do you know?" I asked Prairie. "Where is she?"

"She called me," Prairie said. "From a phone booth. She s-says she's quitting school, too."

"What? She can't quit. It's against the law. Isn't it? It's almost the end of the year. She can't quit now." My brain was combusting, and all the cells were crashing and colliding, just like pins at the bowling alley. She must've been caught. "What happened, Prairie? Did she tell you?"

"Yes," Prairie said. "But she asked me not to t-tell you guys."

"Why?" I said. "We're her friends. We don't care if she's —" I let it dangle. The sentence finished itself in my head: "a criminal."

"I know." Prairie sighed. "She just has some s-stuff to work through."

My head fell against the wall. Poor Max. What if she was convicted? What if she went to jail? What if I never saw her again?

"I'll see you tomorrow," Prairie said. "Maybe we can figure something out."

"Yeah, okay," I said, feeling weak and helpless. "And thanks, Prairie. Thanks for telling me."

"You're welcome," she said.

Since Kevin hadn't arrived yet, I immediately called Lydia and told her. She just kept saying, "Oh, my God. Oh, my God." In the background, Lydia's mother exhorted, "Lydia, please stop saying that. What's going on?"

"I better go," I said.

Lydia got in one last "Oh, my God" before hanging up.

Behind me Mom, Dad, and Vanessa were all standing in a row. Drooling for details. Suddenly it struck me — the reason our family togetherness was getting to me. No one had any privacy. Everyone knew everything about everybody. Not buying Vanessa and me our own phones to speak to our own friends in the privacy of our own rooms was borderline child abuse. Ask anyone.

"What's going on?" Dad asked.

"Nothing." My jaw clamped. "Geez, can't anyone have a private conversation around here?"

The phone rang. I yanked it off the wall. "Hello!"

"Can I speak to Jenny?" Kevin coughed in my ear.

"Uh, speaking." My heart crashed against my ribs.

"What's up?" he asked.

Clutching my chest to keep my heart from heaving right out of the rib cage, I lied, "Not much." The leeches behind me were sucking up every word. Directly into the little receiver holes, I said secretly, "You still coming over?"

"Naw, I can't," he said. "My mom wants me to help my aunt Rachel move some stuff into storage." He hacked again.

My body sagged. "So, what did you want to give me?" I said.

"I can't tell you. Then it wouldn't be a surprise."

A surprise. Oh, boy.

"Kevin, I'm leaving right now!" his mom bellowed behind him.

"I gotta go," Kevin said. "I'll see you tomorrow."

Tomorrow I might be at the jail, visiting an inmate.

After we disconnected, I turned around. Mom, Dad, and Vanessa all had the same sappy smile on their faces. "Not only do I want my own phone," I seethed aloud. "I want my own house, my own car, and *my own life!*"

Chapter 11

Lydia and I both attacked Prairie on the playground. "I d-don't know anything." She fended us off with a stiff-arm.

"Oh, my God." Lydia hyperventilated. "What if she's living on the street? What if she becomes a homeless person? What if she ends up standing on the street corner with a sign that says, 'Will work for food'?"

I curled a lip at Lydia. But the possibilities worried me, too.

Prairie said, "She's not living on the street."

"Where is she?" Lydia and I asked in unison.

Prairie hung her head. Her cheeks turned pink. "I can't tell you. It's a secret."

Lydia was jerking around, whimpering and shaking her hands as if they were on fire. "Get a grip, Lyd." I pulled her hands down. "At least Max is in touch with Prairie and she's okay. Right, Prayer?" I looked at her.

"Right."

"And if Max wants us to know what's going down, she'll tell us. Right?"

"Right. Only —"

Lydia and I stopped and stared at her.

Prairie bit her lip, which had started to quiver. Her eyes welled with tears. "It's not f-fair," she said. "She didn't *do* anything." In a hurry, she hobbled off toward the temp.

"Oh . . . my . . . God." Lydia deflated visibly.

My spirits sank, too. With a thud.

By Friday word had gotten out about Max splitting. You can't keep that kind of stuff quiet. On our way to lunch, Ashley bustled by, purse protuberant, and said, "Busted." She sneered over her shoulder.

I wanted to beat her up so bad. Lydia tried to kick her, but only got air, then fell on her rear. It made everyone around us laugh at Lydia. So what else is new?

After lunch Lydia said, "Look, you guys. We need to talk." Just then Hugh called to Prairie from the bleachers, while Kevin dribbled a basketball over from the blacktop. "Jen, can I talk to you?" he asked.

I looked at Lydia. Made a sorry face.

Lydia exhaled exasperation and stomped off.

Kevin looped an arm around the ball at his side. "What's with Max? I heard she's on the run. Living with homeless people down at the bus station."

My jaw cracked the sidewalk, I'm sure. "Where'd you hear that?"

He shrugged. "Around."

I could just picture Max, pushing around a grocery cart, guarding her meager possessions, and living off Dumpster digs.

"You going to be home tonight?" he said, bouncing the basketball at his side. "I might drop by."

It made me remember he never did give me his surprise.

He added, "I tried to call you last night, but your phone was busy."

Ooh. I'd kill Vanessa. Right after I murdered Dad for talking to Uncle Ralph for an hour. Of course, after Dad's conversation, I was on the phone with Lydia until she had to hang up at nine o'clock on the nose. Then I called Prairie to see if she'd heard anything else about Max, which she hadn't, or couldn't reveal.

"I should be home all night," I told him. Then I remembered — this was Friday. As in, family fun night.

Kevin smiled. "See you," he said.

The smile lingered. See you, too, I vowed. Somehow.

During dinner I persuaded Mom and Dad to move family fun time to Saturday. "It's been a rough week," I told them, which was a mistake because Mom wanted details.

"Nothing specific," I told her. "School is just exhausting. I'm ready for summer vacation. Couldn't we stay home tonight and watch TV together? Maybe go to a movie tomorrow?"

"Fine with me," Dad said, a little too hastily for Mom's liking.

Vanessa looked relieved. Now she could practice her clarinet until her lips turned blue.

At the very same instant, the doorbell buzzed and the phone rang. I raced for the door. The woman standing on the porch, grinning at me, said, "Do you have the Lord in your life?"

"Let me check," I said and closed the door.

Dad came in to take up his usual evening position, lounging in the La-Z-Boy, legs up. "Who was it?" he asked.

"Another Bible bunny," I said.

"Huh?"

Vanessa yelled from the kitchen, "It's for you, Jenny."

Taking the phone from Vanessa, I told her, "I forgot to get a leaflet. Sorry." Turning away from her, I said, "Hello?"

"Jenny, it's me."

My shoulders sagged. Not that I didn't want to talk to Lydia.

"Prairie called," she said. "She told me she talked to Max and she agreed to tell us what's going on. They want to have a Snob Squad meeting tomorrow. I told her we should clear it with you since you're the leader. I have a doctor's appointment in the morning, then I have ballet from two to three-thirty, which my mom won't let me skip, so could we meet after that?"

"Tomorrow," I answered automatically. "Yeah, sure. How 'bout like four?"

A hand clamped over my shoulder. Mom said, "Don't make plans for tomorrow. It's family day, remember?"

"All day?"

"No, just for a couple of hours," Lydia said. "I have to be home by dinner or else I'll get grounded."

I cupped a hand over the phone. "What time's the movie?" I asked Mom.

"We haven't decided what we're going to see yet," she said.

Oh, right. That could take a year.

Mom added, "Just make yourself available."

Geez, is it possible to auction your family off on

eBay? To Lydia I said, "Look, something's come up. I'm not sure I can meet tomorrow."

She clucked. "Does it have to do with you-know-who?"

"Maybe," I lied. "Anyway, why don't you guys go ahead and meet without me. But call me afterwards and fill me in. And tell Max not to quit school."

"Okay, I'll try," Lydia said. "But she won't listen to me. And if she insults me, I'm holding you personally responsible for my actions. Good-bye."

She hung up. A smile warmed me from within. It was good to feel needed. Now the only other thing I needed was for my one true love to turn up.

I hung around the kitchen for a while, opening and closing the fridge, the pantry, the cookie jar. Testing the sharpness of the knives on the rubber dish mat. Watching the clock. After the third trip back from the front picture window, I felt a presence behind me. Dad said, "You're wearing a path in the carpet. I'll come and get you the minute he comes."

"Who?" I said.

He cocked his head.

See? No privacy. I didn't want to confirm the fact that Kevin was actually coming over. "If you don't get me my own phone, I'm . . . I'm going to kill myself." I removed a butcher knife from the chopping block.

Dad wandered across to the fridge. "Don't get blood on the tile grout," he said. "It leaves a permanent stain."

I shoved the knife back in its slot and stormed out of the room. And when a fat girl storms, you can feel the shock waves. Maybe the surprise was that Kevin was kidding. Kidding about coming over. Kidding about liking me. Kidding about any future together. See why I hate surprises?

It might've been the ringing in my ears from my bedroom door slamming, but I swear I heard the phone.

"Jenny!" Dad bellowed down the hall. "It's him."

I raced back to the kitchen. Yanking the phone away from Dad, I rested the receiver against my heaving chest. Dad just stood there, grinning like a goon. "Don't you have somewhere to go, someone to meet, something to launder?" I said to him.

He chuckled and returned to the living room with a bottle of root beer. After hearing the La-Z-Boy creak, I lifted the phone to my ear. "Hello?" I said all breathy, and not faking it either.

"Hey, Jen," Kevin said. "What's up?"

My blood pressure, I almost said. "Not much." My heart raced. "You still coming over?"

"I can't again," he said. "Can you believe it? My mom forgot to tell me we had a birthday party for my cousin Kimmy tonight. She's making me go. But, uh, you busy tomorrow?"

"Tomorrow? N—" My breath caught. All the life went out of me. "Why?"

"I was wondering . . . you wanna, you know, do something?"

Yes! I almost flew through the ceiling. "Like what?" I said.

"I dunno. Go to a movie?"

"Together?" My voice rose an octave.

"No," he said. "I thought we'd go alone. You sit in front and I'll sit in back. I can throw popcorn at you."

I giggled. He was so adorable. "Okay," I said, "but you're buying the popcorn."

With a smile in his voice, he said, "Serious. I could meet you at the mall."

The mall. How romantic. "What time?"

"What movie do you want to see?"

Who cares? I doubt I'd be watching anything after the snack bar commercials. "You pick," I said.

"Okay. How about *Bloody Tuesday: The Amputation?*"

"Yes! I've been dying to see that," I said.

"There's a show at one-thirty," he said. "Or . . ." A newspaper rustled in the background. "Four o'clock."

"I guess the one-thirty. Hold on a minute." Covering the phone with my hand, I whirled around. No

86

one was there, surprisingly enough, so I hollered into the living room, "Dad, could we do our family junk on Sunday instead?"

Mom's head appeared around the corner from the basement stairs. "Would you like to rephrase that?" she said.

"Okay. Can we move our family junk from tomorrow to Sunday?"

Mom gave me her extremely annoyed look. Dad appeared in the doorway. "We all agreed on tomorrow, which, I believe was your suggestion. So, no," he said. "Tomorrow is our family day."

Mom smiled at him. A current of warmth passed between them. Great, I thought. They choose this moment to be joined in holy wedlock.

So much for my first, and last, date. I pounded my head on the wall, hoping for an aneurysm. The blows must've whipped up a brainstorm. "Kevin, you still there?"

"Yeah. What's up?"

"I just remembered, tomorrow is out. Could we do it on Sunday?"

"Sure. Oh, wait," he said. "I can't Sunday. We're going up to my uncle's cabin in the mountains. One of those family things, you know?"

Did I ever. He had a bigger family than the Bradys. I sighed.

He sighed. "I have to see you, Jenny," he said softly. "I have this present for you."

My fingers froze to the receiver. "What is it?" I managed to say without croaking.

"I can't tell you. You know . . ."

"I've never been big on surprises," I informed him. "You can tell me. I'll act surprised."

He was quiet for a long moment. Finally he said, "Naw. I'll just give it to you on Monday."

Monday? Monday was a lifetime away.

Chapter 12

Good thing we had all day Saturday for our family fun time because that's how long it took us to decide on a movie. Mom wanted to see a four-hour-long sweeping epic about some poor family who immigrates to America, strikes it rich, then loses everything and spawns another generation who makes all the same mistakes. Proving that history repeats itself and is as boring as *Barney*. Dad wanted to see a western. Yeehaw. Vanessa didn't want to go, and I voted for *Bloody Tuesday: The Amputation*, thinking I just might run into someone I know and love.

Guess where we ended up? At the latest dorky Disney. The minute we walked in my ears were assaulted by a bejillion screaming kids in the theater. I think their parents dropped them off for the weekend. All the way down the aisle, when my sandals weren't sticking to the tacky carpet, popcorn crunched under my soles. I'd never dig it all out. The only four seats together were on the left side, way in back. It wasn't until I sat down that I discovered my cushion was all wet. I didn't even *want* to think why.

Ever notice how all Disney movies are the same? A beautiful babe and a gorgeous hunk start out hating each other's guts. She saves his life, or vice versa, they fall in love, someone dies then comes back from the dead, and everyone lives sappily ever after. Just like real life — on some other planet.

After the movie Vanessa and I immediately veered out toward the parking lot. Dad called, "What's the rush? Let's mosey on down to the ice cream parlor."

No kidding. He said, "Mosey on down." He said, "Ice cream parlor."

I muttered to Vanessa, "And this is your brain on Disney."

"What's left of it," she muttered back.

"Good idea, Robert," Mom said, looping an arm through Dad's. "It'll give us all a chance to talk."

Vanessa and I rolled our eyes, but we trailed them down the mall. I mean, what could we do? Except try to lose them in the crowd, which was impossible since Mom kept glancing over her shoulder giving us the evil eye.

Near the Nut Shoppe, Vanessa whispered, "This is so bogus. Who goes to a mall on Saturday with their parents?"

"Really," I agreed. "If we see anyone we know, let's start yelling and screaming like we're being kidnapped."

What we did was drop back as far as possible. When we were out of earshot of Mom and Dad, Vanessa said, "So tell me about Kevin."

My face flared. "What do you want to know?"

"Where did you meet him? What's he like? Does he have a brother?"

I said, "At school. He's way cool. And I don't know."

Van shook her head. "I can't believe it. My baby sister has a boyfriend before I do."

"I'm not a baby," I replied. "Unless you're talking baby elephant."

"You just turned twelve. I bet you don't even have all your permanent teeth yet."

I sneered. "I'm going on thirteen. I have permanent teeth *and* PMS, for your information."

She stared off down the mall and sighed. "Who'd want a sicko like me, anyway?"

I stopped and grabbed her bony arm. "Don't say that, Van. You're not a sicko."

She just looked at me.

"I mean it. You're lots better. When was the last time you cut your Cheerios in half?"

A smile tugged the corner of her lip.

"See?" I said. "And you hardly ever get lost in mirrors. Or change your clothes a hundred times a day — wait, that's normal. Oh, I know. You hardly ever take more than two or three hours in the bathroom to count the hairs in the brush. Just that one time I had to go so bad that I ran out to use the tree in the Crotchedys' backyard."

"You didn't —" She shoved me. I shoved her back.

"Hurry up, you two," Dad called through cupped hands. "You're losing us."

"He noticed," Van murmured.

We resumed our funeral procession toward the ice cream parlor. Out of the blue Vanessa said, "Dr. Sid wants me to open up more; express my feelings. So here goes. I'm glad you're my sister."

I looked over at her, shocked. "Ditto," I managed to say.

She added, "And believe it or not, as weird as they are, I'm glad they're our parents."

"Yeah, I wouldn't want to wish them on anyone else. Well, maybe Ashley Krupps." Speaking of *witch* . . . the pink Nikes caught my eye first. Then the too-tight jean skirt, the velour top, and the purse. The purse that was strapped to Ashley's chest like an oxygen tank.

"Quick, hide me." I spun Vanessa around and ducked behind her. As if a walking stick could hide a tree trunk. Using Vanessa as a shield, I watched Ashley and Melanie approach.

Vanessa slowed. "Keep walking," I whispered, twisting her around in a half circle.

"It's kinda hard when you're pulling me backward," she said. But she got my drift and wove in and out of traffic.

Finally they were past us and I loosened my death grip on Vanessa's arms. Geez, it left welts. "Sorry," I mumbled. Peeking over Vanessa's shoulder, I watched as Ashley wiggled her rear and gestured dramatically to Melanie.

Vanessa said, "Who are they?"

"Just some snobs from school —" Snobs! I had to call the Squad. This was our chance to catch Ashley in the act. No doubt she was here to spend Mrs. Jonas's money. Then I remembered: Ashley had been hanging around near the PC lab that day, too. She could've taken Ms. Milner's money. And if I had to choose between Ashley and Max as far as criminal tendencies, Ashley got my vote.

"Come on." I grabbed Vanessa's wrist and yanked. "We need to find a phone."

Chapter 13

Vanessa suggested an alternate plan. She said she'd stall Mom and Dad at I Scream Ice Cream while I went in search of a phone. Luckily, I had some change on me. Luckily, I remembered Lydia's number. Unluckily, no one answered. "Come on, Lyd," I pleaded to the coin slot. Three, four, five rings.

"Hello?"

"Yes! You're there," I said.

"Where else would I be?" Lydia grumbled. "Mom won't let me go to Max's this afternoon."

"Why not?"

Lydia sighed wearily. "She heard about the thefts at school. She called Mr. Krupps and I guess Max's name came up." She clucked. "He told her Max was seen at school the day Ms. Milner got robbed."

Who would've told? . . . Ashley, I seethed silently. She must've spotted Max. The snitch.

Lydia went on, "I guess Mr. Krupps sent the cops to Max's house, but she got away before they could handcuff her and read her her rights."

Lydia was prone to exaggeration, but it made me shudder to think it might be the truth. My resolve to get Ashley Krupps registered off the Richter scale.

Lydia said, "Now my mom doesn't want me hanging around with Max anymore."

"But Max didn't *do* it." At least, I didn't think so. I hoped not. I wanted to believe so bad. . . .

"I know she didn't do it," Lydia replied. "But try telling my mother that."

No way. You don't disagree with a child psychologist. She has the power to pack you off to the funny farm, wherever that is. I didn't think it'd be funny. "Look, I'm here at Creekside Mall and I just saw Ashley and Melanie. This is our chance. If we can catch them spending the stolen money, we'll have proof Ashley did it and Max didn't."

"Yeah, perfect," Lydia said. "But . . ."

I waited. "But what?"

Lydia sighed again. "How can we prove the money they're spending is the stolen money?"

Good point, I thought. Too bad Prairie wasn't here. She'd know the answer, since she's the brainpower of the Snob Squad.

"Well," I thought aloud, "we could at least see how

much they're spending. I bet it'll be almost exactly what was stolen. Then we report it and let Krupps take it from there." Oh, the gossip. The humiliation. The lifelong grounding. What a delicious thought.

"Not bad," Lydia said. "But what do I tell my mom?"

Geez, did I have to do all the thinking? "Tell her whatever you have to. Then call Prairie. Tell her to get hold of Max and meet us —" I glanced around, "in front of the Sears in half an hour." I didn't figure we'd run into Ashley anywhere near Sears. "Be here by four o'clock. Same time we would've met at the Peacemobile."

"This is a waste of time," Lydia muttered.

"It's our best opportunity to prove Max's innocence." Prove it to myself, I didn't say. "Don't you want to get her off?"

Lydia clucked. "Of course I do. I just meant . . . my mom . . ." She exhaled. "I'll see what I can do."

A few minutes later I sauntered casually into I Scream Ice Cream, squeezing through the narrow aisles between tables, and elbowing some old lady's head. Mom and Dad glared. Mom especially. "Where've you been?" she said. "We've been here for ten minutes. There's a line of people outside waiting for these tables."

"Sorry." I almost added, Call the ice cream cops. "Did you order already?"

"No," Mom said. "We were waiting for you."

I studied the menu. Everything was color-coded. No fat. No sugar. No dairy. No eggs. No taste. Finally, at the bottom was the real deal. I ordered a peanut butter parfait with extra nuts and whipped cream. Mom opened her mouth, then shut it when I shot her my most defiant stare. Sometimes it works.

My food diary loomed in my mind. "Okay, forget the extra nuts," I told the waitress. "And the whipped cream." That seemed to please Mom.

Dad made chitchat while we waited. I kept twisting around, looking at the clock. By the time our ice cream arrived, it was ten to four.

You know how when you eat ice cream in a hurry it makes your head throb? Instant headache. I bet when my brain burst and splattered gray matter all over the wall, the tables would clear out fast.

Mom said, "Maybe if you ate slower, you'd enjoy your food more."

"Who says I'm not enjoying it?" I slurped a heaping teaspoonful of parfait into my frozen wasteland of a mouth. "In fact," I added, just to irk Mom, "I could probably enjoy another one."

Vanessa smirked. That encouraged me. "Or even two," I said, "by the time you guys finish. Could you hurry up?" It was now three minutes to four.

"What's the hurry?" Dad said. "We're just sitting

here enjoying each other's company. Aren't we, hon?" He took Mom's hand.

Vanessa and I rolled eyes. "Yeah, well, the people in line aren't too thrilled about our family hour."

I thumbed over my shoulder, where a mob of moms with screaming kids machine-gunned us down with dirty looks.

"What else do we want to do today?" Dad asked.

"I'm glad you asked," I said. "Personally, I'd like to stay and shop. Since we're here."

"Good idea," Mom said. "I need some new pantyhose. And Robert, you could use a few new pairs of boxer shorts."

Panic surged. My eyes met Vanessa's. Her panic mimicked mine. Suddenly Van fell forward, clutching her stomach.

"Vanessa, what's wrong?" Mom said.

"I feel sick," she replied weakly. "I might have the flu. It's going around. I haven't felt good all day."

"Why didn't you tell me?" Mom said.

Vanessa shrugged. "I didn't want to spoil our family fun time."

That's when I knew she was faking it.

Dad stood. "We'd better get you home."

Mom helped Vanessa to her feet. "That's the trouble with this family," Mom said. "We don't communicate." She looked at me.

Why was she looking at me? I thought I communicated what I wanted very clearly.

We weren't even out of our chairs before there was a stroller stampede toward our table. "Yeow!" I cried when a twin double-seater smashed my foot.

The mad mom didn't even apologize. And I swear the little brats gave me matching evil grins.

Outside the ice cream parlor, Vanessa stopped and said, "I don't want to spoil everybody's fun. We don't *all* have to go home."

"Nonsense," Mom said. "Of course we're all going. We wouldn't be a family without you."

Vanessa heaved a sigh. "There's no reason Jenny has to come. She could stay and shop. And, I just remembered, I do need a new clarinet reed. Could you get one for me, Jen? A Mitchell Lurie Premium, three and a half." She cocked her head at me pathetically. "I need it by tomorrow." She coughed.

"Sure, Van. No problem," I said, like I knew what she was talking about. Squeezing her shoulder, I added, "You just take it easy. But if you don't make it, could I have your CD player?"

She almost laughed, then covered it in another cough.

I looked at Dad. He opened his mouth, but before he could speak, I said, "I'll be all right. You can pick me up in a couple hours. I'll call you when I'm ready." I answered Mom's unspoken objection with, "I won't be alone. I saw a couple of friends earlier. I'll catch up with them."

She lived to hear I had friends. It made me seem normal.

Vanessa groaned. "Could we go now?"

Dad's eyes met Mom's. Somehow, silently, they settled the debate. Dad dug in his wallet. "If you happen to be in Penney's, near the men's underwear —"

I snatched the twenty. "Not in this life," I muttered.

He chuckled as he slid an arm around Vanessa's waist. Before they disappeared into the sunset, Vanessa twisted around and smiled at me.

For a sister, she was way cool.

Chapter 14

Lydia and her mom, Dr. Marianne Beals, were waiting in front of the Sears store when I got there, huffing and puffing my guts out. I'd met Dr. Beals when the Squad had a sleepover at Lydia's house to take glamour photos, and I liked her a lot. For a mom. Lydia's complaint was that she was a control freak. But whose mother wasn't?

"Hello, Jenny," Dr. Beals said. "How are you?"

"Fine," I wheezed. Before I could ask about the others, Lydia said, "Prairie is going to meet us here." She held a finger to her lips, so I knew not to ask about Max.

"These thefts at your school are unconscionable," Dr. Beals said to me, like I knew what that meant.

"Yeah, I know," I said, like I did.

"Lydia tells me Max is innocent. That you think you know who did it, but don't want to accuse anyone until you have proof. I think that's admirable."

My face flared. Did I say that? Lydia was full of it.

Dr. Beals added, "Even though I really feel you should tell your principal what you know."

"Mother, please." Lydia rolled her eyes at me. "I can handle it. That's what you want me to do, right?"

She didn't have a comeback for that.

"Yo!"

We all turned. Saved by the Max. She and Prairie materialized out of the crowd. Boy, was I glad to see Max alive and kicking. Lydia rushed over to greet her, leaving me alone with Dr. Beals, who'd gone stiff as a board.

It wasn't just Max's appearance. Or maybe it was. Max was sporting a black sports bra with her baggy camouflage pants. The pants hung halfway down her hips and you could see the plaid waistband of her boxer shorts. No one ever accused Max of *not* making a fashion statement. No one ever accused Max of anything, if they valued their life.

Lydia grabbed Prairie's arm and hitched her chin at me. "I'll call you when we're done," she yelled over her shoulder to her mother.

Leaving Dr. Beals in the dust, we hauled you-know-what down the mall. "You're not really quitting school, are you?" Lydia asked Max.

"Maybe," Max mumbled.

"Have you really been living at the bus station?" I said. "With the homeless people?"

"Huh?" Max curled a lip at me.

"Can I tell them?" Prairie said.

Max shrugged. "I guess."

"She's b-been staying with me. Her mom knows and everything."

"Thank God." Lydia slapped her chest.

"So, what happened with the cops?" I asked.

Max replied, "I'll tell you later. Where's Krupps-butt and Melon-head?" We'd stopped and gathered 'round the wiener wagon.

"They were heading toward Dillard's," I said.

"What's the plan?" Lydia asked.

Why does she always ask me? Oh, yeah. I'm supposed to be the leader.

Max said, "It's obvious, isn't it?" She looked at Lydia like she was a helium head. To me, she said, "Prayer thought we could use these." She shoved her hands into her extra-large pockets and pulled out four plastic cases.

As she passed them out, I cried, "Brilliant, Prairie!"

Prairie blushed. "My brothers got them for Christmas."

"What are they?" Lydia asked, examining her black box.

Prairie answered, "Walkie-t-talkies."

A slow smile spread across Lydia's lips. "I get it. For spying. Sweet."

Prairie added, "They might need batteries."

I pressed the Talk button. "Breaker, breaker," I said into the microphone. "This is Sumo Sal calling any ears on in the SS. What's yer flying orders, good buddies?"

Max's eyes widened. "You know CB?"

"My uncle Ralph was a trucker. About six jobs ago. He taught me."

"Cool," Max breathed. I felt a new reverence all around. "Teach me to say, 'Roger, Charlie. Over and out.'"

I pressed my Talk button. "Roger, Charlie. Over and out."

Max gave me her death look.

"Or you could say, 'To ya, buddy. On the flip-flop.'"

Prairie giggled. She pressed her button and said, "On the f-flip-flop." It echoed out into the mall.

Lydia tried her walkie-talkie. Nothing happened. "Mine's dead," she said.

Max tested hers. It was dead, too. "First stop," I told them, "is the Walgreens for batteries."

On the way I informed them that we needed to

make up handles. "You know, code names. Like Seat to the Saddle; that was Uncle Ralph's. Or Lady Lead Foot. That was his girlfriend's."

"Cool." Max shook her head. "This is so cool."

Sometimes I loved being the leader. When we got to the cashier to pay for the batteries, Lydia said, "I didn't bring any money. Did you?"

Max and Prairie dug into their pockets. They had about thirty cents between them. "I'll get it," I said, even though I was planning to spend that twenty on replenishing my stash of candy. With low-fat granola bars, of course. "I'm rich today."

A knowing look passed between Max and Prairie. I didn't know what it knew. "What?" I asked.

Prairie lowered her eyes. "Nothing," she said.

I shrugged it off. Weirdness ran rampant in this group.

As we loaded the batteries and headed down to Dillard's, I taught everyone a few phrases in CB talk and we tried out our new handles. "Breaker, breaker," I said to my box. "This is Sumo Sal, coming in on the south side. Anyone got their ears on? Over."

"That's a five five," Max said. "What's yer flying orders, Sumo?"

"Spy in the sky." I covered my mike. "That means a helicopter cop, but it could mean just a spy, too.

Puttin' the kill on the Krupps. Reckon to turn her over to the big hats." Which means catching Ashley in the act and letting the authorities know, loosely translated.

Lydia pressed her Talk button. "Carmen SanDiego here," she said. "Over."

We all looked at her.

"What? She's the only spy I know."

Prairie signed on. "This is Double O T-Trouble. Here's pie in your eye." She grinned.

Max raised her walkie-talkie to her mouth. "Roger, over. This here's La Cucaracha." She grinned.

Only Max would dub herself The Cockroach.

"There they are!" Prairie pointed. Quickly she raised her walkie-talkie to her lips. "S-Suspect headed into World of Leather."

"Over," Lydia replied. "Let's go."

"Wait." I grabbed her sleeve. "One of us goes in. The others hang back. Spread out. Take cover."

"I'll go in," Lydia said. She dashed toward the door, then stopped and spun around. Pressing her walkie-talkie close to her mouth, she said, "Can you hear me?"

Her voice came out loud and clear. Max replied, "You're supposed to say, 'Breaker, breaker.'"

"Excuuuse me," Lydia said. It echoed in the mall.

"Be careful, Lydia," I said.

"Sorry," she whispered.

I added, "Check in when you get close to them. Try to find out what they're buying and how much it costs." I told the others, "Let's split up. Keep the World of Leather in sight."

We all headed off in different directions. I crouched beside a potted palm, while Prairie and Max slipped behind the giant fountain.

A few seconds later my walkie-talkie crackled to life. "They're leaving," Lydia's voice whispered through my box.

"They buy anything?" I asked.

"Negatori," she said.

Another voice came on. "Suspects headed to Pamela Petites," Prairie said.

Max replied, "I got 'em."

"Stay close," I ordered everyone else.

Reflected in the stores' glass panes, Lydia slinked down the mall. If she wasn't careful, she'd be picked up by the mall police for suspicious behavior. Max's voice came online. "They're looking through the shorts. Wait. Krupps is taking one to the fitting room."

Lydia said, "Like Ashley could get one leg into a pair of petites."

Prairie tittered.

"La Cucaracha," I called. "What's Melanie doing?"

"Nothin' much. Standing around, acting stupid.

She's got a bag from Blockbuster. Looks like a CD or something."

Rats, I thought. We missed a purchase. Okay, she'd spent probably twelve to fifteen dollars on the CD. "Keep watching," I ordered Max. "If Ashley picks anything out, go back to the rack and see how much it costs."

"That's a five five," Max said.

We repeated the routine four more times. One of us would follow them into the store and note the prices on anything they bought. We were so good, so invisible, I considered adding covert operations to my list of career possibilities.

It was after six o'clock by the time we trailed Ashley and Melanie to the exit. The four of us walkie-talkied our way to the food bazaar. Lydia called her mom to tell her she was eating with us; reassure her she wasn't being corrupted. Meanwhile, I bought a pepperoni pizza and we jammed into a booth.

"Okay," I began. "I figure they spent about . . ." I counted all the places they'd been on my fingers, trying to remember all their purchases.

Lydia said, "Here, I wrote everything down." She withdrew a little spiral notebook from her pocket and flipped it open. "Give me a minute to add it all up."

"Lyd, you should be a Boy Scout," Max said.

Lydia gave her a dirty look.

Max swallowed her mouthful of pizza. "What I meant is you practice their motto: Be prepared."

She met my eyes.

"It's a compliment," I said. "Isn't it?" I queried Max.

She smirked. Lydia went back to eating and calculating. "They bought those matching sleeveless T-shirts for eight ninety-nine each, and the earrings, and those hair scrunchies."

"Don't forget the CD," I said.

Prairie piped up, "Did you guys notice that Ashley p-paid for everything?"

My eyes widened. "You're right, she did." That should add fuel to the fire. The fire with which we were going to burn Ashley Krupps to a crisp.

"It comes to forty-eight dollars and ninety-nine cents," Lydia announced. "Give or take five dollars for the CD. Who knows if it was on sale or not?"

"So, let's say fifty bucks," I said. "Assuming they already spent Mrs. Jonas's money on their matching outfits, how much was stolen from Ms. Milner?"

Everyone looked blank.

"I could ask her on Monday," Prairie said.

Lydia added, "And if it's more than that, we could always follow Ashley again next weekend. This was fun." She beamed.

We all beamed. It'd been a blast.

"All right," I said. "By Monday afternoon Ashley's

going down. And it won't be in a blaze of glory. Which means, Max, you'll be in the clear."

"Who cares?" she grumbled.

"I do," Prairie said.

"Me, too," I said. We both looked at Lydia.

She clucked. "Of course I care."

"All for one," I began.

"And one for all," they finished. We gave the Snob Squad salute.

Chapter 15

Kevin was waiting for me Monday morning when I got off the bus. Falling into step beside me, he said, "How are ya, Jen?"

I almost melted all over his Reeboks. "Good," I said casually. "How was your uncle's cabin?"

"It was okay. I, uh . . ." He grabbed my arm and swung me around to face him. His eyes darted back and forth, searching for anyone within earshot. Such as Lydia, who was hustling toward us at the speed of a spitwad. Luckily she tripped over her feet and crashed into a trash can, which rolled into another one creating a domino effect all the way to the Dumpster. Leave it to Lydia.

Kevin said quickly, "Iwantedtogiveyouthis." He pressed something into my hand. It was a box, white and oblong, held together with a red rubber band. "Ididn'thavetimetowrapitsorry."

"Another present?" I stared at the box. "Geez,

111

Kevin. You shouldn't have." Then I thought, Why not? I'm worth it. I sounded like a shampoo commercial and it made me giggle.

Kevin smiled. "Go ahead. Open it."

I turned the box over. On the bottom was a price tag. I gasped. Out loud I read, "Ninety-five dollars and ninety-nine cents?"

"Huh?" Kevin's jaw jammed. He read the sticker and blushed. "Sorry," he mumbled. "You weren't supposed to see that." He tried to scrape it off with a thumbnail and couldn't.

I had the urge to hug him, but checked it.

Rolling off the rubber band, I lifted the top and gasped again. "Oh, my God, Kevin!" Inside was a glittering gold chain with a little gold *J* in the middle. It was dainty and delicate. And expensive-looking.

"You can wear it all the time," Kevin said. "It's real gold. It won't turn green in the shower or anything."

Just then Lydia arrived. "Hi, Jenny. You'll be glad to know Max is back."

"All right!" It was looking like our last week of school was going to be awesome.

"Oh, hi, Kevin," Lydia said dryly. "I suppose you two love birds want to be alone."

Neither of us replied.

"What's that, another present?"

Without answering, I looped the necklace over my

head. The little links flowed through my fingers. I'd never felt anything so precious, so perfect.

Lydia punched her fists into her hips. "Okay, fine. Be a snot. Act like Ashley." She huffed, then spun and stomped away.

That hurt. "Lydia, wait," I called.

She didn't turn around.

"Lydia!"

Kevin said, "I gotta go, anyway," He hoisted his backpack onto his shoulder. "The guys are waiting. Maybe we could do a movie or something this weekend."

"I do," I said. "I mean, I'd love to."

"Yeah?" He smiled. "Okay."

Kevin passed Prairie on her way down the sidewalk. "J-J-Jenny, I g-gotta t-t-talk to you," she said, scurrying over. She must've been excited or anxious, her stuttering was so noticeable.

"What's up?" Over her shoulder, I watched Kevin ambling away. Even from the back he was adorable. Lydia had already disappeared around the corner.

Prairie sniffed. That got my attention. She looked like she was going to cry.

"What's wrong?" I said.

"Oh, Jenny." Her eyes welled with tears. She exhaled a shaky breath. "I just found out how m-much m-money was stolen from Ms. Milner."

"How much? More than fifty dollars?"

She nodded. "A lot more. Almost a hundred dollars."

My Cheerios coagulated in my stomach. Something dropped from my now-limp fingers. A box. An oblong box with a price tag attached.

By lunchtime Lydia had forgiven me. It took a note of apology wrapped around my last roll of Smarties, but it was worth it. "When are we going to turn Ashley in?" she asked. "I typed up all her purchases so Mr. Krupps could read it. The total, with tax, comes to fifty-four dollars and ninety-five cents, give or take five dollars."

Prairie met my eyes. Tried to. Mine were busy scraping the Formica, while my new necklace seared a chain-link noose around my neck.

"What?" Lydia said, noticing the silence. "Oh, I know it's not as much as she took. She just hasn't spent it all yet. We'll have to keep following her until she does."

"At this rate we could be following her forever," I muttered.

Lydia blinked. "What do you mean?"

Prairie piped up, "Almost a hundred dollars was stolen from Ms. Milner."

Lydia looked from Prairie to me and gulped. Shaking my head, I said, "That makes like two hundred dollars altogether. We don't have nearly enough evidence to take to Mr. Krupps."

Prairie smiled at me. "Thank you, J-Jenny," she said.

For what? I wondered.

She added, "You're a good person, down deep."

Quit it, I thought. You're going to make me cry.

"But everyone knows she did it." Lydia's voice rose.

"Yeah, but we have to have more proof. At the moment nothing adds up." And I wasn't just talking numbers.

Prairie wanted to meet after school, so we rendezvoused at the third-base dugout to walk to Max's house together. Everyone was quieter than usual. I don't know what they were thinking, but I was wondering how I'd made it through the day. The whole six and a half hours was one big blur. I didn't even remember what I ate for lunch, which is scary. It might indicate brain damage. Mostly I was trying *not* to think what I was thinking, except every time I started to zone out, this gold chain burned another notch in my neck.

As we scrambled up into the Peacemobile and took our seats, Prairie said, "It was really rotten to steal from Ms. Milner. She's my favorite teacher."

"Yeah, she's cool," Max said. "You got anything to eat, Solano?"

"How can you think about food at a time like this?"

Max arched eyebrows at me. Everyone did. Proof. Brain damage.

I dug in my pack. The only thing in there was half an Oreo left over from who knows when. Might've been last year. "Sorry," I said. "The cupboard is bare." As I pulled my hand out, it caught on something. The something flipped out and landed on the floor.

Prairie picked it up. "What's this?" she said.

Lydia replied, "Kevie-poo gave Jenny another present."

They all *ooh*ed. Instinctively my hand reached up to cover my throat.

"I saw it," Lydia said. "It's a gold necklace with a little *J*. Show them, Jenny."

My cheeks sizzled. I wished I had a Hostess Cupcake to dam up Lydia's big mouth. "It's probably not real gold," I muttered.

Max pushed up from her beanbag chair and clomped over. She ran the chain through her fingers and whistled. "Nice."

Prairie studied the box. "For ninety-five dollars and ninety-nine cents, it b-better be."

I snatched the box back.

Lydia said, "Touch-ee."

"Shut up, Lydia," I snapped.

She flinched. At any moment she was going to burst into tears and I'd have to slit my throat. But when they buried me, the necklace was going, too. "I didn't mean that the way it sounded," I said. "It hasn't been a very good day."

"It sure h-hasn't," Prairie said. "I also found out that the stolen money was from our S-Save the Starving Orphans in India fund."

All eyes widened at Prairie.

She went on, "All this year we've been raising money to send to India. I'm sure I told you that."

"No, you didn't," Lydia barked.

I frowned at her. Don't take it out on Prairie, I thought. Hooboy. Stealing from a teacher was one thing; stealing food from starving children was another.

The Peacemobile grew somber. We all stared at the rusty floor. Except Lydia. I noticed her eyes were glommed on my neck. Instinctively I shoved the necklace back inside my blouse and said, "Didn't Hugh give you a necklace, too, Prairie?" Maybe they were two for the price of one, like the earrings.

"No," she said. "Like I told you, he d-doesn't have much money."

"Well, Kevin must be loaded," Lydia said.

Why couldn't she just drop it?

Prairie stood up. "Somehow we've got to get Ms. Milner's money back."

"How?" Lydia said to my face. "Looks to me like it's already been spent."

That did it! I stood to leave. Prairie caught my arm. "We don't really know who took it," she said. "And we probably n-never will unless they confess, which would be the Christian thing to do."

My eyes strayed out the cracked front window. A magpie swooped over the junkyard and screamed. I knew how it felt. As my eyes grazed down the dusty dashboard, they caught on the cracked vinyl driver's seat. And what was sitting on it. "Hey, is this new?" I lumbered over. "Let's play some music."

"What is it?" Lydia peered over her glasses.

Max got up and grabbed it from me. "What's it look like?" She shoved it in Lydia's face.

"A CD player," Lydia said. "I got one just like it for my birthday."

"Well, whoop-dee-do," Max said. "I had to buy mine."

"Or steal it," Lydia snorted. The rest of us didn't think that was so funny at the moment.

Max spun around and said, "I know how we can get Ms. Milner's money back. I could sell this."

We all stared at her. Was she serious?

"It cost fifty-six bucks, but if I threw in some CDs, I bet I could get seventy-five or eighty at the flea market."

"No way," Prairie said. "But . . ." She paused. "That isn't such a bad idea. Does anybody else have s-stuff to sell?" Prairie looked at me.

"Don't look at me," I said. "My CD player's about a hundred years old. We'd be lucky to get fifty cents."

Lydia said, "You and Prairie could sell your earrings."

We both reached up at the same time to protect our treasures. Lydia added, "Or that necklace."

Prairie cut off my lunge for Lydia's throat. "What would I tell Hugh? He probably spent his life savings on these earrings."

To Lydia, I said, "You must have something to sell. You're rich."

All the blood rushed to her face. "No, I'm not," she mumbled, adding in a small voice, "not that rich. Anyway, my mom would kill me if I sold the birthday present she gave me."

"Why? It's yours now. You know what, Lydia? You let your mother make all your decisions for you," I told her.

"I do not!" Lydia cried.

"Cut it out," Max interrupted before fisticuffs

broke out. "This is stupid." She wrapped the electrical cord around her CD player and added, "The flea market's Saturday. Case closed."

I felt all eyes on me. Prairie, especially, was glaring daggers. "What?" I said.

"Are you going to let her d-do that?" she asked.

"No," I said, just to say something. "I mean, Max." I turned to her. "You don't have to. Not unless you . . . think you should."

Prairie stormed over to the door and wrenched it open. "I'm going home," she said.

Max growled at me.

"What?"

She stomped across the van and followed Prairie out. Sticking her head back in, she snarled, "If you want my brother to take you home, you better get your rear in gear. He doesn't have all day."

When they were gone, the Peacemobile closed in like a tomb. "Geez," I said, more to myself than Lydia. "What's with them? What's with everybody?"

She scoffed. "As if you didn't know." She got up and left, too.

Outside, the magpie screeched. Inside, I did a perfect imitation.

Chapter 16

Dear Fickle Friends and Fried Food Diary,

I don't remember what I ate for lunch. Or breakfast. Just add a thousand calories. For dinner I had mashed potatoes, a buttermilk biscuit, and two of the Colonel's extra crispy, extra spicy chicken wings. Add three thousand more calories. Afterward I still felt hungry. Or empty.

What am I going to do? My life is a soap opera. Which wouldn't be so tragic if I was getting paid to star in it. But this is no act. Someone close to me is a thief. I'd like to believe it's Ashley Krupps, but to tell you the truth, there's no more evidence against her than either Max or Kevin. The only person I can eliminate at the moment is me. So how come I'm feeling so guilty?

I'll tell you why. Because it's really crummy to suspect your friends, like you don't even trust them. Especially your sort-of boyfriend. What if

he's a crook? What if he isn't? That would mean
Max is. Know what's double crummy? If I had to
choose, I'd rather Max was guilty so I could still
love Kevin. Isn't that awful?

A knock sounded on my door. "Don't come in," I hollered. There was one last line I had to add.

Nothing I could eat would make me feel better.

"You have a phone call," Vanessa said through my door. "It's Kevin. Or Max. They sound a lot alike."

Another wave of guilt washed over me. "I can't come to the phone right now. I'm . . . sick." At heart.

Vanessa opened the door.

"Hey!" I covered my chest with a pillow, even though I wasn't naked or anything. Just felt that way.

"You okay?" she said.

I shrugged.

"You want to talk about it?"

"No." Tears welled in my eyes. "I don't think I can."

She studied me. "I'm here if you need me."

All I could do was nod.

There was a welcoming committee to greet me as I stumbled off the bus the next morning. Kevin, Lydia,

Max, Prairie, Hugh. They all had the same sappy smiles on their faces, as if I'd just won the Powerball and they were my nearest and dearest friends. Which they were.

Kevin moved up beside me. "Want me to carry your backpack?" He reached for it.

"No, that's okay." I yanked it back. "I don't want to give you a hernia."

He chuckled and wrenched it away from me. No kidding, we had a tug of war. Don't ask me why I didn't want him to carry it. Maybe because I hadn't had a chance to write down breakfast in my food diary, so I'd tossed the notebook into my pack to update during language. Which, I realized too late, was a huge mistake. The memory of what happened last time someone saw my food diary still mortified me. If anyone saw *this* stuff . . .

Prairie scurried by and whispered, "I don't know when you did it, but th-thanks."

I frowned. "Did what?"

She smiled and elbowed me.

On the way in we passed Ashley and Melanie, gossiping outside the door. Ashley clutched her purse closer to her chest. Double weird. She still had my vote as most likely to be committed.

Mrs. Jonas hadn't even finished the hot lunch count

before the door flew open and the stench of Old Spice hit my nose. Mr. Krupps's beady eyes bounced around the room. "I have an announcement," he said.

Everyone dummied up.

He pursed his lips and stared over our heads. I turned to see what he was staring at. The only things back there were the restroom and drinking fountain. My gaze met Max's and she rolled her eyeballs back into her head. It made me giggle, which reverberated in the silent space. Krupps said, "Yesterday, Ms. Milner's money magically reappeared in her desk."

That shot my head back around. I glanced over at Prairie. She bit her lip and dropped her eyes. On the other side of her, Hugh was nodding his head. Kevin leaned around him and smiled at me. Instinctively my hands came together. Then again. I clapped.

From the front row Ashley turned around and glared. I proffered her a hand gesture I'd learned from Max.

"That's not all," Mr. Krupps said. "This morning she found even more money in her desk. About twice as much as was stolen in the first place."

I gasped. I wasn't the only one.

He added, "And there was another envelope with twenty dollars and an IOU for the rest."

My eyes zoomed in on Prairie again. This time she was staring back at me. Lydia twisted around from her desk in front to widen her eyes at us. I spun around to catch Max's reaction. She sat sprawled in her desk, sucking sunflower seeds.

"So," Mr. Krupps went on, "I find this all very interesting. Fascinating, in fact. Apparently we're having a run on Good Samaritans. Now, if one of you is the thief, I'm sure we'd all be eternally grateful if you'd return Mrs. Jonas's money, too. Wouldn't we, Mrs. Jonas?"

Her cheeks lit up like lanterns.

"In fact," Krupps said, "I might even consider forgetting the whole ugly business. This time." His eyes zeroed in on Max, who choked on a sunflower shell. "Think about it," he barked and headed for the door.

"Mr. Krupps?" Lydia's voice stopped him.

He pivoted in place. "Yes?"

"Why don't you give the extra money to Mrs. Jonas? That seems fair."

He blinked, like the thought hadn't occurred to him. "I'll think about that," he said. "Thank you for the suggestion. This still doesn't clear you." *You*, as in Max. He stalked out.

General mayhem ensued. It took the threat of rescinding recess for the rest of the school year to get us under control. I don't know about anyone else, but I felt fantastic. This was great. Problem solved. Now I could forget I ever suspected my friends.

It was Lydia who had to bring up the one annoying little loose end. We were at lunch, spreading out to eat and share, when she said, "Wow, Ms. Milner must've gotten back an extra three hundred dollars. Or will with the IOU." She shook her head. "I can't believe people who didn't even take the money are returning it."

Prairie said, "Maybe they're trying to protect the real thief."

"I doubt it." Lydia opened her pudding cup.

"Why?" Prairie said. "Wouldn't you do that for a friend?"

Lydia snorted. "It'd have to be a really good friend."

It grew quiet, except for the chewing. I guess we were thinking about that. Me especially. Would I cover for a friend? Yes, on one condition. I'd have to know which friend it was.

Chapter 17

Dear Forever Fat Unless I Fast Forever Diary,

I'm giving up food. It's the only way I'll ever lose weight. I hate my body. If you could see me in shorts, you'd hate my body, too. I hate myself more. Especially when I cheat, the way I did after school when I ate a supersize Snickers bar without blinking. Why can't I control myself?

Minnette says I don't have to give up all my favorite foods, just eat in moderation. I say she's whacked, except that's how she lost about a hundred pounds and became a registered dietician. Registered dietician does not even make my list of top one hundred career possibilities.

Minnette says I have to learn how to control my appetite. But once I start eating, I can't stop. It's depressing.

That's not the only thing I'm depressed about. It's summer and I want to wear shorts. Every-

*one is, even Ashley. But if Kevin Rooney ever
saw my thunder thighs, he'd run so far so fast.
He might figure out the J in my name stands for
Jumbo.*

*You'd think keeping Kevin as my boyfriend
would be motivation enough to make me stop eating. More than anything in the whole wide world
I want to be tall and thin and gorgeous. I already
failed tall. Vanessa got those genes. And as for
gorgeous, I can't even get close with a glamour
photo. Even Kevin said I looked better in my natural state. Which is why I really like him. Really
really. I might even love him. For real.*

*Which is also why I refuse to believe that he
had anything to do with the thefts at school. And
if he did, which he didn't, it was just a mistake
and he put the money back.*

*But he didn't do it. And neither did Max. But
if she did, and I'm not saying she's guilty, she
would've put Ms. Milner's money back, too. Or
left the IOU.*

*I wish I'd have thought of an IOU. I bet Prairie
gave some of the money back in the name of
friendship for Max. Not that Max did it.*

*Oh, man. If I had another supersize Snickers
bar I'd snarf it down right now. It's all so de-*

*pressing. I wish I knew the truth about my
friends.*

The next day at school Prairie pulled me aside before
the bell and told me Kevin wanted to ask me something. My heart stopped.

My first thought was, He's going to ask for the
necklace back. He wants to return it for the money.

Prairie smiled and whispered, "Say yes."

I frowned. "To what?"

She wiggled her eyebrows. "It's a surprise."

Oh, goodie. Another surprise.

Needless to say I couldn't concentrate on daily oral
language. Not that I ever could. Every so often, like
six times a second, I sneaked a peek at Kevin. Whenever I caught him looking at me, he smiled. I melted.

He could have the necklace back. He could have all
my jewelry. Vanessa's and Mom's, too. I'd sell my
soul for Kevin Rooney.

It wasn't until we were heading out to lunch recess
that Kevin caught my arm and whispered, "Meet me
out by the bleachers." He sprinted off.

For the first time ever, I didn't run after him. I
stalled around in the restroom, combing my hair and
arguing in the mirror with my conscience. So what if
he's guilty? I reasoned. A lot of prison inmates get

married. And look on the bright side. I'll always know where he is at night.

When I finally arrived at the field, Kevin was standing, scraping gravel around in a circle at his feet. He looked up and smiled. "Here." He handed me a package.

"Please." I pushed it away. "No more presents."

"It's just gum," he said. "You want a hunk?"

My cheeks seared. "Sure," I said.

"Hugh and I wanted to know if maybe you and me and him and Prairie could get together. You know, do something."

I unwrapped my Dubble Bubble and tossed it into my mouth. Highly illegal. Highly delicious. "Sure," I said. "When?"

Kevin blew a bubble and it popped. He sucked it in. "I was thinking Saturday night. We could rent a movie. Maybe order a pizza or something."

A memory flashed into focus. "Hugh's favorite pizza is anchovy," I said.

Kevin looked like he was going to hurl. "Did I say pizza? I meant Chinese take-out."

I giggled.

He smiled.

"Sounds like fun," I said. "What time?"

"I don't know. Seven?"

"Seven it is." Oh, brother, I sounded like Miss Manners.

"I don't live too far from you," Kevin said. "Just a few blocks." He told me his address. I pretended I didn't already know it.

"Hugh said his mom could pick you up on their way over, if that's okay."

"Yeah, that'll work," I said.

"Did you know he lives right next door to Prairie?" Kevin shook his head. "How lucky can you get?"

Lucky as Lucky Charms, I almost said. Fortunately the bell cut off that retard remark.

"Geez, already?" Kevin glanced at his watch. "Let me finish this, then I'll walk you in." With his right Reebok, he scraped something in the dirt.

I focused on his feet. The circle he was scraping earlier wasn't a circle. It was a heart. Inside the heart, he'd scraped *K+J*.

In a futile effort to get my heart restarted, I swallowed my gum.

Chapter 18

Dear Fantasy, Fun, and Flavor-Filled Food Diary,

He loves me. He loves me. He loves me. Oh, yeah. Today was a good diet day. I had three bites of Dad's magic meatloaf, which was chewy as chicken gizzards. One more bite and I would've barfed my green beans. Which, believe it or not, were actually tasty. I even had a second helping. And I passed on dessert.

P.S. Did I mention Kevin Rooney loves me?

"Jenny and Vanessa, your dad and I figured out something to do for our family fun time that we'd all enjoy," Mom said, as Vanessa and I were settling in to watch reruns of *Beavis and Butt-Head.*

Dad stood behind Mom in the doorway, his arm snaking around her waist.

Vanessa looked at me. Neither of us dared ask.

Dad grinned. "I'll give you a hint. Yo, ho, ho, and a bottle of rum."

Vanessa's eyes grew wide. "We're cruising the singles bars down by the dock?" She looked interested.

Mom said, "No." She clucked at Vanessa. "Pirate's Cove. It opens this Saturday for the summer."

Vanessa choked. "Are you insane? Nobody plays putt-putt anymore."

Mom folded her arms. "You never like any idea we come up with, Vanessa. You're so negative. That's part of your problem; part of *our* problem as a family. Nothing we ever try to do pleases you. At least Jenny's willing to give our family fun time a try."

Which made me choke. The last thing I wanted to do in the world was humiliate myself in public again.

Mom added, "I'm probably going to have to work Saturday, so we'll go Saturday night."

Saturday night? The remote control slipped out of my hand and clunked across the coffee table. As I retrieved it, I imagined what was going to happen after I told Mom what I was about to. Walking the plank came to mind. Mutiny came to mind. "Uh, gee, I'd really like to go to Pirate's Cove for a few rounds of family putt-putt, Mom, Dad." I smiled at them. "But, uh, I already have plans Saturday night."

All eyes zeroed in on me.

"Are you going out with Kevin?" Van asked. She

realized her error before my eye bullets assassinated her.

To divert disaster, I huffed and said, "I kept Friday night open because I know it's family night. Then you go and change it on me. Geez."

Mom lowered herself into the La-Z-Boy. "Just what were you and Kevin planning to do Saturday night?"

"Oh, I don't know. Smoke dope and have sex."

"Jenny!" Mom almost dislocated her jawbone.

Dad cracked up. Propping himself on his elbows behind Mom, he said, "You can have sex, but don't do drugs."

"Robert!"

Van and I both cracked a smile.

Mom stared me down. "Well?"

My smile faded. "He asked me to come over and watch a movie. With Prairie and Hugh. Geez," I said again. Like it was a mortal sin to hang out with your friends.

"So much for putt-putt," Vanessa said. She took the remote from me and clicked on the TV. As she channel surfed to MTV, she said, "Don't do anything I wouldn't do." In a murmur, she added, "Like I'll ever get the chance."

From the end table, Mom retrieved the *TV Guide* and flipped through it. "I'd like to get to know this boy better. Why don't you invite him to dinner before your date?"

In this life? "We were going to order out. Chinese gourmet or something." I glared at her.

"How are you getting to his house?" Mom glanced over the *TV Guide* at me.

Why didn't she turn off all the lights and dangle a naked lightbulb over my head? "Hugh's mom is taking him and Prairie and picking me up on the way."

Vanessa bounded to her feet. "Anyone want popcorn?"

I raised my hand. So did Dad.

"No." Mom leaned back and propped up her feet. She blinked at Vanessa. "I mean yes to popcorn, no to Jenny."

My head whipped around. "What do you mean 'no'? You mean I can't go? Mom, I'm almost thirteen years old. I'm the oldest person in the world to never have a date. Besides Vanessa."

From the doorway, Van's eyes nailed me.

"Sorry," I muttered. "Mom, if I don't go, he won't ask me again. You don't know Kevin. He's the most popular guy in school. Girls would do anything to get a date with Kevin Rooney."

"Anything?" Dad arched an eyebrow.

"Pretty much," I answered.

"That's the problem," Mom said. "I don't know him. And I didn't say you couldn't go. I just think he should come and pick you up himself." Her finger traveled down the page of TV shows. "It's only good manners," she said. "That way, I, we" — she looked up at Dad — "can spend a little time with Kevin."

"Oh." My fit fizzled. "Okay." A little time, as in a split second.

"Well, then, it'll be just the three of us for family fun night." Mom sighed. "Let's watch *Providence*."

I might've groaned. The microwave dinged and I followed my nose to the kitchen.

Vanessa stood at the counter, arms folded.

Guess she heard. "I owe you one," I said.

"A big one," she said. "A gigantic, mammoth, enormous, unbelievably big one."

"Okay." I rolled my eyes. "I get the picture."

We had seventh-grade orientation the next day in school. If you made it to seventh grade at Montrose, you got rewarded by being able to choose your own classes. Not all of them; you still had to suffer through math and English and reading, but you could take a few electives, too. Such as chorus and French and domestic sciences, which was basically cooking and cleaning and caring for any children you might have unexpectedly.

Orientation was supposed to get us hyped about coming back to school after summer break, but all I felt was fear. Not that it wasn't exciting to be in seventh grade, finally, after all the build-up. But it was scary, too. Like crossing over into adulthood. Coming of age. Making life choices. Kindergarten was starting to look good in retrospect.

As we were transferring between classes, I said to the Squad, "What happens if you take the wrong electives and end up skilled in something like auto repair?"

Max's eyes gleamed. "Is that a choice?"

"Don't get excited." I held her down. "I was just giving an example."

She deflated like a flat tire.

Lydia said, "Personally, I'm taking art and music and dance. All the fine arts. Since I plan to be an actress."

We looked at her.

"What?" she said.

"Nothing," I said. "At least you have a career in mind. The only thing I can picture myself doing is working the counter at Wendy's."

As if out of fairy dust, Kevin materialized at my side. "What are you going to take, Jen?" he asked.

"I don't know," I answered. "I don't see sumo wrestling on the list." I cringed. Why did I say that?

He laughed and punched my arm. "Let's try to get at least a couple of classes together, okay?"

"Okay." Seventh grade was looking up.

"I really want to take computer lab," he said.

"Oh, me, too," I lied.

"And I guess, since we have to take a science class, I'd like biology. I hear you get to dissect frogs and stuff."

"Great." I gagged. "Wow, you're picking all my top choices."

He beamed. "Let's compare schedules Saturday night."

"Uh, speaking of Saturday." I gulped. "There's been a change in plans."

He stopped dead. I skidded to a halt and turned around. "Come on, Jenny." Lydia tugged at my sleeve. "We're going to be late to geography."

Geography? Who needed that? "You go ahead. I'll catch up."

Kevin watched Lydia, Prairie, and Max tromp off down the hall before blinking back to me. "You mean you can't come?" He sounded disappointed.

Quickly I answered, "Oh, I can still come."

Did he exhale in relief? I think he did.

"It's just that my parents want to meet you. They said you should pick me up." I smiled wanly.

Kevin shrugged. "Okay. Should I wear a suit and tie?"

"Do you have a suit of armor?"

He laughed and punched my arm. I hoped the burgeoning bruise would never heal.

Lydia slid in next to me at lunch. She was steamed about something. You could see the smoke swirling out of her ears. When she stabbed a chunk of meat like it was crawling off the tray, I said, "What's up, Lyd?"

"You wouldn't believe what Ashley did today!" she screeched.

I emptied what was left of my eardrum into my palm. "Why don't you tell us?"

Across the table, Max and Prairie stopped eating.

Lydia let out a short breath. "I can't talk about it. Not yet. Not here. I'll tell you later, in the Peacemobile." She shook her head and her eyes narrowed. "We've got to get her. We've *got* to."

While she stewed over her chicken-fried steak, Prairie and I discussed our upcoming date. "What are you going to wear?" Prairie asked.

"I was thinking about borrowing my mom's black negligee," I answered.

Prairie giggled. "Do you think it's too c-cold to wear shorts?"

My eyes widened. Prairie was the only other girl in school besides me who wouldn't wear shorts. She wouldn't even wear a skirt, since it exposed her prosthesis. But Hugh was fascinated by Prairie's fake foot. He'd probably love the opportunity to study it up close and personal.

Unfortunately I didn't think showing off my cellulite would advance Kevin's and my relationship beyond Saturday night. "It might get kind of chilly," I said, "depending on how late we stay out. Maybe we should just wear jeans."

"Okay," Prairie agreed. "My grandma got me this cashmere sweater on her trip to Ireland. It has little pearls in the neck. Do you think that'd be too dressy?"

"Do you mind?" Lydia snapped. "I'm trying to eat."

Prairie's eyes held mine. We both zipped our lips, literally. I wondered if we shouldn't elect a class for Lydia. Something called uncontrollable anger management.

Chapter 19

After school we stopped at 7-Eleven for snacks before heading to the Peacemobile. The only thing I could find that remotely resembled diet food was a bag of pork rinds.

Settling into our places, I opened the bag and said, "Know what I'd do with two hundred dollars? I'd have liposuction. They ought to be able to suck out twenty pounds of fat for two hundred dollars." I crunched into a pork rind and retched. "It'd sure save me a lifetime of dieting."

Max said, "I keep telling you, Solano, you're not fat."

Lydia interrupted. "Does anybody care what Ashley did to me today?"

"Hey, Lydia," I said, passing her the bag. "Are you ever going to tell us what Ashley did to you today?"

She snatched the bag from me, sneering. Picking out the curliest pork rind off the top, she said, "You wouldn't believe it if I told you."

"Try us," Max said.

Lydia snapped off an end, chewed, and swallowed. She held out her hand to Max. Max passed her the liter bottle of Pepsi One we were sharing. Lydia wiped the rim with her finger.

"We don't have all day," I said.

Lydia blinked at me, then took her sweet time slugging down half the bottle. If I wasn't such a benevolent leader . . .

Lydia gave the bottle back to Max, who passed it on to Prairie. "We were in domestic sciences," Lydia began.

"I'm taking that," Max broke in. "That will be sooo fun."

We all stared at her. The moment of shock passed.

Lydia went on, "I was asking Ms. Ramos about the unit on personal appearance and hygiene because I heard from some seventh graders that we got to have our colors done."

"Our what?" My nose wrinkled.

"Our colors. You know, learning what makeup and clothes go best with our skin type and personality."

"I'm signing up tomorrow," Max said.

I couldn't tell if she was joking or not. The only colors she ever wore were camouflage and black.

"Anyway," Lydia said as she wound her hair behind her ears, "before Ms. Ramos could answer me,

Ashley yells out from the back, 'We already know your colors, Lydia. Black and blue.'"

"Oh, brother," Prairie muttered.

"I know," Lydia said. "Even though it wasn't funny, everyone laughed. Especially the seventh-grade attendants who were showing us around. Then Ashley said, 'Hear that siren? I think it's the fashion police. They're coming for you, Lydia.' Which made everyone laugh louder."

I shook my head sympathetically. Even though Lydia did wear some strange getups, like pink flowered shirts with green plaid shorts, that kind of public humiliation was uncalled for. Even from Ashley.

"Krupps is a cow," Max said.

"Thank you, Max," Lydia replied. She took the bag of pork rinds from Prairie as it made its return trip. "She's still wearing that purse like it's a vital organ."

"I was thinking more like a tumor," I said. "A tumor on the world, which is what she is."

"Thank you, Jenny." Lydia handed off the bag to me. "Whatever she's got crammed in there has got to be illegal."

"It's got to be the stolen money, or what's left of it," I said.

Nobody answered. The only sound was crunching pork rinds.

"It's probably a carton of Camel cigarettes. Isn't that her brand, Max?" Lydia said.

"How would I know?" If Max could blush, she would have.

"Hey, Max," I said. "Why don't you just casually walk by tomorrow and rip Ashley's purse off her arm. Too bad if her arm comes with it."

Max's eyes lit up. Everyone hyena howled.

"I think we j-just need to figure out a way to get Mrs. Jonas's money back." Prairie looked at me.

"Don't look at me," I said. "The only thing of value I own are my earrings and this gold necklace from Kevin. You'd have to kill me to get them."

"How do you want it?" Max asked. "Awake or asleep?" She grinned evilly.

"Ha, ha." I sneered at her, but decided I'd leave the light on tonight.

Lydia said, "I still think the extra money Ms. Milner got should go to Mrs. Jonas."

"I don't," Prairie said. "People gave that m-money back for the starving orphans of India. It wouldn't be right to give it to Mrs. Jonas." She turned to me. "Can't you think of anything, Jenny?"

I frowned at her. "No." Geez, being leader didn't mean I had all the answers.

"Let's play some music," I said, to change the subject. "Go get your CD player, Max."

"Can't," Max said.

"Why not?" Lydia asked.

Max slurped the last sip of Pepsi and crushed the bottle under her foot. "Hocked it," she said.

Prairie gasped. "You sold your new CD player? Why?"

Max shrugged. "Needed the cash."

Lydia asked, "How much did you get?"

"With all my CDs included, almost a hundred bucks."

"So," I ventured cautiously, "what did you do with the money?"

Slowly Max turned to me. "One guess."

I gulped. "Starving orphans?"

She didn't say yes and she didn't say no. The one question I really wanted to ask, I couldn't. All I could do was stare at her shoes.

After that we sort of ran out of things to talk about. Next to me, Lydia sulked on the sofa. I think she was still steaming over Ashley. Prairie kept looking at me, not saying anything. I think she wanted to discuss our upcoming date and couldn't in Lydia's presence. Across from me, Max lounged back in her beanbag chair, eyeing my necklace and earrings. It made me nervous, so I got up and said, "Well, I better get going. I have gobs of homework." Right. On orientation day? The obvious lie only intensified the silence.

"Plus," I added feebly, "I need a sugar fix and these pork rinds just don't hack it."

Everyone exhaled and got up to leave.

"Wait, guys, before you go." I blocked the door. "I want to ask you a question."

All eyes focused on me.

I took a deep breath. "Say someone you knew, a friend, did something bad, for whatever reason. Would you ask them about it? Just to know why? Because you'd probably understand if you knew why. You'd forgive them because they were your friend."

They all stared at me, vacant-like.

Finally Prairie said, "I hope I w-wouldn't have to ask."

I looked at Max. She nodded, but didn't volunteer a confession.

Prairie added, "I'd hope this person would trust us enough to tell us the truth."

Again, my eyes honed in on Max. Nothing.

Lydia was playing deaf-mute, too. I think she was so convinced of Ashley's guilt, she was blind to other possibilities.

The silence grew again until it became staggering. I hated it; this air of mistrust that hung between us. At last, Max spoke. "You never really know a person, do you?" she said. Her eyes bore into mine.

"No," I said back. "I guess not."

Chapter 20

Friday morning I woke up with a swarm of bees in my stomach. It was the weirdest sensation. Not queasy, the way you get before some dreaded event. This felt more like anticipation, thrill, eagerness. And not because today was the last day of school. Today had to fly so tomorrow would come. Tomorrow night, to be exact, when my first summer romance would begin.

The framed plaque Dad had hung over the toilet about a hundred years ago captured my attention while I brushed my teeth. It read, *Today is the first day of the rest of your life.* What do you know? I thought. It's true.

Prairie, Lydia, and Max were all waiting for me when my bus screeched to the curb. First thing Lydia said was, "Thank God this year is over. It's been the worst year of my life." She pushed her glasses up her nose and blinked. "Except for the Snob Squad," she added.

Our eyes all met and we smiled. Automatically we gave the Snob Squad salute.

As if summoned, Ashley and Melanie strutted by on their way to the temp. Ashley said, "Hey, the fashion police must've released her on bail."

Melanie added, "In that outfit, I'd bail, too."

Ashley screamed with laughter.

Max stepped out and threatened them with a fist. They scurried inside. "I hate her," Lydia said. "What's wrong with this outfit? My mom just bought it."

I didn't say what I was thinking. Mothers should never pick out clothes.

"You look fine," Prairie said. "She's just j-jealous."

Lydia scoffed. "What do I have that she doesn't have?"

I counted on my fingers, "A brain, personality, intelligence, friends."

Lydia didn't hyena howl, the way I expected. She looked like she was going to cry. Quickly I added, "And a future in show business."

"Yeah, right." She shook her head. "Who am I kidding?"

Along with Lydia's anger management class, add building self-esteem. Maybe we could all use that class.

Kevin sprinted over from his basketball game. Panting, he said, "I'll come by around six-thirty tomorrow night. Okay?" He positioned himself in front of me and started walking backward.

"Make it six forty-five," I said. Barely enough time to say hi and bye. I didn't want my mother to get her claws into Kevin, or Dad to start discussing the pros and cons of bleaching boxer shorts.

"Sounds good." Kevin smiled. "See ya, Jen." He dribbled off. My bees had babies.

"Hugh and I'll just meet you there," Prairie said.

"What time's this orgy start?" Max asked. "Maybe me and Lyd'll crash the party." She grinned at me and elbowed Lydia.

"Forget it," Lydia said. "I have better things to do with my time."

"Like what?" Max asked. "Clip your nose hairs?"

Lydia glared at her. Without a word, she stomped off.

"Good job, Max," I said.

"Hey, I'm sorry." Max shot me a dirty look. She called to Lydia, "Leave 'em long if you want."

Lydia wrenched open the trailer door and stormed inside.

"What's with her lately?" I asked. "Permanent PMS?"

Prairie shook her head. I guess she'd noticed, too. Lydia was so testy lately. Something was bugging her. Or some*one.*

And it didn't take a brainiac to figure out who. Right after roll, Mrs. Jonas said, "We're going to see a movie this morning. But first I want all of you to clean out your desks. Up on the book rack are folders of papers for you to take home. Whatever's in your desk that never went home can also go in the folder. The projects I want to keep for the PTA are up here behind my desk."

Lydia's diorama wasn't among them. I saw her spine go rigid and knew this was not going to improve her mood one bit. Of course, it was partly her fault since she never bothered to put the diorama back together after hurling it across the room. Ashley had just sort of thrown stuff in there. On the report cover was the A minus Mrs. Jonas had given Lydia on the project, which I thought was pretty generous, considering. Luckily, Lydia didn't ask me what I thought.

Mrs. Jonas went on, "There are plenty of trash bags and Comet and sponges in the back. This temp room needs to be spotless. We're starting summer school classes in here on Monday. And please, people, let's keep the noise level to a low roar."

The room exploded in activity. I saw Ashley get up with her purse and head to the restroom, which wasn't unusual. She spent half her life in there. On the way, though, she bumped into Lydia's desk and sent her backpack flying. All of Lydia's trashy romance novels tumbled out. "Oops." Ashley pressed a fat finger to her mouth like it was an accident.

Before Lydia could gather them in, Melanie picked up a paperback and gasped. She handed it to Ashley. A smile spread across Ashley's face. "Mrs. Jonas," Ashley said as she pivoted, "Lydia brought pornography to school."

In a flash Lydia yanked Ashley's purse off her shoulder and raced down the aisle. Ashley screamed, "Give it back!" and chased Lydia. Max hollered, "Over here, Lyd!" Lydia tossed the purse into Max's outstretched arms. Crashing through desks like a raging elephant, Ashley groped for the purse. Max threw it back to Lydia. It all happened so fast, no one had time to react. Mrs. Jonas might've said, "Cut it out," but who was listening? This was too funny.

Max and Lydia continued their game of keep away to the front of the room with Ashley wailing and flailing behind. I didn't see who opened the purse, but suddenly its contents were scattering all over the floor. Items began bouncing around: lip gloss, eyeliner, hair clips, keys, her wallet, a package of Kools. But that wasn't the interesting stuff. A can rolled down the aisle and clunked into my desk leg. Even before I picked it up, I knew what it was. One whole cupboard at home used to be filled with cans of it. Slim-Fast.

Ashley actually body slammed Lydia, who retaliated with kicks and slaps. I heard Mrs. Jonas yell, "Stop it, you two!" But like a volcanic eruption, it was too late to stop what had been building between them all year.

Lydia grabbed the purse from Max and spun away. As she turned back, she said, "What have we here?" She held up a little velvet box. The light reflected off something shiny inside. "Gold earrings. Fourteen-*karat* gold," Lydia exclaimed. "I wonder how much *those* cost."

Snatching her purse back, Ashley wheezed, "Those aren't mine."

"Prove it." Lydia smiled.

Ashley charged Lydia again. Just in time, Mrs. Jonas stepped between them. She snapped, "Lydia, give those back. And both of you sit down. Now!"

Ashley whirled to face us. Her eyes looked panicked as they scanned the room, wild and helpless. I knew then it wasn't the earrings that had drained all the blood from her face. The cigarettes either. It was the cans of Slim-Fast people were picking up from under their desks. Those and the boxes of Dexatrim.

Ashley could hardly breathe as she scrambled around the room, collecting everything and shoving it back into her purse. Everyone was laughing — the boys, especially.

My heart ached for Ashley. I got up and went over to help, but when I handed her a can of Slim-Fast and said, "Chocolate Royale's my favorite flavor, too," she yanked it away from me so hard, her ragged fingernails drew blood. Ashley's eyes met mine. Hers welled with tears. "Ashley —"

"Shut up!" she screamed. "I hate you." To the room, she screeched, "I hate all of you!" Then she hugged her overflowing purse and charged out of the room, leaving the door flapping in her wake.

Melanie hurried past me.

"Mel —" I began.

The hatred radiating from her halted me midsentence. She flew by, trailing Ashley out. Behind me Max muttered, "Busted."

No kidding. No doubt Ashley would run straight to her father and report Lydia. Report all of us. We might not be back for seventh grade.

Mrs. Jonas looked straight at me. I couldn't hold her gaze. Instead, I blinked up at Lydia. Her face was frozen in shock. Slowly she sank into her seat. In a tiny voice she whimpered, "Ashley started it."

Mrs. Jonas said, between clenched teeth, "The

movie's off. Just get busy and clean out your desks. And I don't want to hear another word out of anybody the rest of the morning."

All I could do was shake my head. Lydia didn't get it. But I did. I felt Ashley's pain.

Suddenly Lydia jumped up and raced to the restroom. The door hadn't shut all the way before we heard her sobbing. I guess she did get it.

After "the Ashley incident" the bees in my belly turned to wax. Even though I expected us to be spending the last day of sixth grade on suspension, or expelled from Montrose Middle School, it didn't happen. Ashley never came back to class. And she must not have reported us, either, because Mr. Krupps didn't break down the door in a rage.

By lunchtime I figured out why we were still in school. Ashley couldn't go to her father, not with incriminating evidence in her purse. Cigarettes were bad enough. I doubted Mr. Krupps knew about her diet pills and Slim-Fast, either.

Poor Ashley. All this time I thought she was oblivious to her weight; that it never bothered her, the way she just threw it around. If things were different, if we weren't such mortal enemies, we might've been able to talk. There's an invisible bond between those of us forced to live fat in a skinny-is-the-only-thing-beauti-ful world.

I don't know if it was just because I was feeling sorry for Ashley or what, but I wasn't convinced she was involved in the thefts. The secret stash in her purse wasn't stolen money or merchandise. Just secrets. Ashley was a liar, a snot, and a cheater, but I'd never known her to be a thief.

Which sure made Max's shoes gleam brighter in the light of day. Almost as bright as my earrings and necklace. As hard as I tried, I couldn't stop suspecting Max and Kevin. Where did Max get the money for those shoes? Where did she get the money for a new CD player? It was apparent from her ramshackle house that she didn't live in the lap of luxury.

Kevin, on the other hand, might. He'd have to be rich to afford to buy me such expensive presents. Maybe he lived in a mansion with a pool and servants. Maybe his parents were forcing him to go to public school so that he could mix with the lower classes. It almost made me want to cancel tonight. Almost. But now I felt compelled to go, to see his house. Because even though it could change everything, it was time to learn the truth.

Chapter 21

I managed to squeeze into my white jeans with an inch or two to spare, but I still looked like an albino rhino. My hair chose tonight of all nights to revolt against styling gel. It fell in curly clumps to my shoulders. "Maybe a hat," I thought aloud.

As I scrounged through my closet for my old Brownie beret, Dad called down the hall, "Jenny, he's here."

I squealed. Six forty-five on the button. Not only was Kevin a prime suspect, he was punctual. With one final swipe at my hair in the mirror, I stumbled blindly out the door.

Mom had Kevin skewered to the La-Z-Boy, while she and Dad grilled him from the sofa. "What do your parents do for a living?" Mom asked.

Vanessa stood in the doorway, sucking on a clarinet reed. She rolled her eyes at me.

Really.

I had to rescue him. "Kevin doesn't have parents," I said, motioning him to get up and follow me to the front door. Which he did, at rocket speed. "He's from Venus."

Dad said, "I thought men were from Mars, women were from Venus."

Mom whapped him. Smiling at Kevin, she said, "Sit down. Stay awhile. You, too, Jenny." She patted the cushion next to her. "What's the hurry?"

She had to ask?

Mom quizzed Kevin about school and hobbies and sports, while I died a slow, agonizing death. Dad was worse. He just sat and stared at Kevin, studying him like he was bacteria under a microscope.

Mom said, "What's your phone number, Kevin? I might give your mom a call."

He rattled off his number so fast, Mom had to ask again. When she told Dad to get her a pencil so she could write it down, that was my cue. I got up, grabbed Kevin's sleeve, and yanked him out the door, slamming it so hard the house shook.

"Sorry about that," I told Kevin as I hustled him up the block. "Five more minutes and you would've been strip-searched."

He laughed and elbowed me.

I added, "Are your parents that weird?"

"Weirder," he said. "It's just my mom, though. My dad's gone."

"Gone where?" I asked.

"Who knows?" he answered. "He forgot to write."

Which pretty much ended that line of questioning. As we turned onto Yancy Street, a warm finger snaked into my hand. Then another. Then all of Kevin's fingers laced through mine. The bees were reborn. They ripped through my stomach and swarmed up my spine.

We didn't talk the rest of the way. We didn't have to.

Hugh and Prairie were just getting out of the car when Kevin and I reached his house. This was his house? Surely they'd gotten the address wrong. It was nowhere near a mansion; not even a whole house. More like a duplex; two units glued together by a garage.

This didn't seal his guilt. I mean, the Rooney mansion could be undergoing major renovation. Right? This could be temporary housing.

A lady rushed out the door of the duplex and said, "Oh, Kevin, good, you're home. Listen, your aunt Rachel called and wants me to go out with her for a drink." She tousled his hair.

He smoothed it back into place before mumbling introductions. His mom scanned me from head to foot. By the shock in her eyes, I could tell she wasn't bowled over by my beauty. She punched the garage-door opener and said, "I don't know when I'll be back. Behave yourselves."

"Oh, you bet," Kevin said under his breath while squeezing my hand.

My stomach lurched. And it wasn't all from thrill. This could be the shortest date in history. What if my mother really called? Could Kevin do an imitation of his mom? Could I? And the more worrisome question: What if Mom didn't call? My stomach fluttered again.

"Make yourselves at home." Kevin motioned us through the door. He kicked an overflowing laundry basket aside. "It's kinda messy."

Kinda? Pots and pans were piled high in the kitchen sink. Dirty dishes covered the counters — I assumed there were counters under there. It made me appreciate my dad's housekeeping skills.

"The movies are under the TV." Kevin pointed. "What does everyone want on their pizza? Besides anchovies." He winked at me. I couldn't help it; I swooned.

"I don't care," Prairie said.

"Cheese," Hugh said.

"Duh." Kevin widened his eyes. I sucked in a smile. "Jen?" he said.

I loved the way he said, "Jen."

"Anything but anchovies," I answered.

"You got it." He followed the phone cord through a mess of papers on the table. While he called in our order, I wandered over to help pick out a movie.

As Hugh started through the stack, Prairie pulled me aside. "Look what Hugh g-gave me," she said. Her fingers spread out in front of my face. On her left hand was a ring. I think it was a ring, even though it was rectangular and odd.

I bent down for a closer look.

"It's an old computer chip," Prairie explained. "Hugh made it himself." She traced her fingers over it tenderly.

"So, is the wedding going to go live on the Internet?" I asked.

"Jenny." Prairie pushed me playfully and blushed.

"Okay, I've narrowed it down to three movies," Hugh said.

This should be good, I thought.

He carried the tapes over to the sofa and sat. Prairie sat beside him. Kevin was still on the phone, on hold, so I sank in next to Prairie. Sank doesn't begin to describe it. The sofa was soft as a featherbed. In fact, it might've been a featherbed. There was a pillow at one end and a crumpled blanket at the other. A thought suddenly occurred to me. What if this is Kevin's bed? Oh, my God. I might actually be sitting on Kevin's bed.

Hugh said, "*Halloween: H20.*"

"Oh, yeah," I said.

"No way," Prairie countered. "I hate scary movies."

Kevin appeared out of the sea of laundry and sat down beside me. Right beside me. And he kept sinking and sinking until we were both almost horizontal. I scrambled to right myself.

"Okay, how about *Terminator II?*" Hugh said.

"That's the best one," Kevin said.

"It's t-too violent," Prairie said. "What's the third choice?"

"*Armageddon,*" Hugh said.

Prairie's eyes lit up. "That's my favorite movie."

Destruction of the world isn't violent?

Kevin said, "Here, I'll put it in." He got up, causing me to slide into the sinkhole he'd vacated. As Kevin switched on the VCR and stuck in the tape, Hugh asked, "How much is the pizza?" He dug in his pants pocket for his wallet.

"Forget it," Kevin said. "My treat."

"Really?" Hugh poked his glasses up his nose. "Gee, thanks."

"No problem," Kevin said. He grabbed the remote control and pressed Start.

Hugh asked, "What'd you do, rob a bank?" He cracked himself up.

Kevin didn't answer. The FBI warning scrolled onto the TV screen as the hairs on my neck stood at attention.

Kevin plopped down beside me again and fast-forwarded through the previews. When the movie credits appeared, Kevin got up and switched off the lights. On the other side of me, Prairie snuggled close to Hugh.

Kevin's leg landed right next to mine. He took a deep breath. My breath was stuck somewhere between my lungs and lips. Out of my peripheral vision, I saw Hugh's arm slide around Prairie's shoulders. He leaned over and kissed her.

Kevin said in my ear, "I just got pepperoni."

I jumped a mile. The reflection from the TV flickered over Kevin's face. His adorable, smiling face. I smiled back. "Great," I said. "I'm starving." And to prove it, my stomach rumbled.

"Me, too." Kevin stretched his arms over his head. One of them cruised across my shoulders.

My bones went brittle. Don't ask me why; I'd been waiting for this moment all my life. Not that Kevin could feel my bones under all my layers of blubber, but I tried to relax. When I'm nervous though, my impulses take over. I blurted, "So, is this Mrs. Jonas's treat or Ms. Milner's?"

Kevin's arm dropped back behind me. "What do you mean by that?" he said.

"Nothing," I answered quickly. Oh, God. Did I really say that?

Suddenly the overhead light flashed on. Kevin faced me. "Did you just accuse me of stealing the money?"

"No." I looked aghast. "Kevin, no. Of course not." I gulped. "But, uh . . . did you?"

"Jenny!" Prairie barked at me.

"What?" I turned to her. "I didn't say he did. I'm just asking."

Kevin folded his arms. "Do you think I did?"

My eyes met his. His very intense eyes, holding mine in a vise grip. "No." I hope not, I managed to keep to myself. "I just . . ." My mouth tasted like bee vomit. Involuntarily, my fingers traced across the links of my necklace. "It's just that right after the money got stolen, you gave me these presents. I mean, it was pure coincidence. First Mrs. Jonas's money and the earrings. Then Ms. Milner's money and the necklace. Weird." I laughed. It sounded strangled, which it was.

All the warmth in Kevin's eyes faded away. My life

went with it. An explosion from the TV rocked the living room. Kevin raised his arm to flick off the TV with the remote control. Just then the doorbell buzzed.

Beside me, Prairie said, "Jenny, how could you?"

"I —"

The whooshing of the door cut me off. Kevin snarled at the pizza guy, "You must have the wrong house." He shut the door in his face. Then he turned to us and said, "The party's over."

Chapter 22

Dear Fat Fink Forget About Food You Stupid Idiot Diary,

He hates me, he hates me, he hates me. I'm gonna eat some worms.

I threw my food diary across the bedroom, where it landed with a splat over my fat white jeans. I let out a wail that could be heard in Vail.

Good thing Mom, Dad, and Vanessa weren't back from family fun night. They weren't here to see me stumble home alone in the dark and almost bust my bed frame when I flung myself on it so hard.

Even if Kevin would've walked me home, the look on his face after I accused him of stealing the money was enough to make me flee for my life. With one stupid remark, I'd managed to destroy any future we might've had together.

When the tears started, they wouldn't stop. I'd

never felt so miserable in my life. All my diet days added together couldn't come close to the feeling of emptiness I had inside me right now. My one chance at love, flushed down the toilet.

Through my sobbing I heard someone enter the house. Yes, I thought. Good. An ax murderer. Counting the footsteps in the hall — four, five, six — I quickly axed the ax murder scene. Blood makes me queasy.

A soft knock sounded on my door. "Jenny?" Mom whispered softly. "Are you home?"

I yanked my comforter up to my chin. A streak of light shone through a crack in the door and I shut my eyes. From the hallway, Mom said, "She's here. Thank God. She's asleep."

I wish. And thank God for what? I'll be here the rest of my life, I thought. I'm never getting up. How can I ever show my face in public? Even Prairie had pierced my heart with a look that killed. And after Kevin tells everyone what a snake I am . . .

Why did I have to ask him? Why did I have to know?

"Jenny?" Another sliver of light cut across my bed. I clutched my covers tighter. The light expanded before a body bounced on the bed. "How'd it go, Jen? I know you're not asleep." Vanessa shook my arm.

"Go away," I snarled.

She climbed over my lifeless carcass. "Tell me

everything that happened," she said to my half-covered face.

"Nothing happened," I grumbled.

"Did he kiss you good night?"

No, he kissed me good-bye, I answered to myself. Throwing her off me, I rolled over and muttered, "Can't you see I'm trying to sleep?" Can't you see I'm trying to die?

"Come on, Jenny. Tell me."

"Go away, Van." My voice cracked. "Leave me alone."

She sank down beside me and rested her head next to mine. "What happened, Jenny? Are you okay?"

No. And I'm never going to be okay. To Van, I said, "I don't want to talk about it."

"Jen—"

"Just go!" I shouted at her.

"All right." She bounced up. "God." She padded to the door. "Excuse me for caring." The door slammed.

Sunday morning I was awakened by an earthquake. When my eyes flew open, I realized the only thing shaking was my bedroom door. "Jenny, are you deaf?" Dad bashed it again. "I've been calling you for ten minutes." The door creaked.

"Don't come in!" I cried. "I'm naked." Covering

my head with my pillow, I added a muffled, "And deaf, too."

"You have a phone call," he said.

There was no one in the whole wide world I wanted to talk to. Lifting the corner of the pillowcase, I murmured, "Who is it?"

"One of your many admirers."

That didn't even warrant a reply.

Dad strolled into my room, carting the laundry basket.

"Did I say 'Enter'?" I threw off the pillow.

He said, "You know, if you'd fold your clothes and put them away, it'd save me a couple of loads of laundry a week." He tossed my white jeans and a pair of underwear into the basket.

That got me up. "I'll do that," I said. "Just go."

He sighed and headed for the door. "The phone?"

"I'm coming," I snarled. Geez, he sounded more like a mother every day. Maybe it wasn't healthy for a dad to play Mr. Mom. Too much gender bending.

I threw on my robe and padded down the hall. A knot of fear clenched my stomach. What if it was Kevin? Then a surge of hope loosened the knots. What if he was calling to apologize? What if everything was back to normal? What if last night never happened?

My hand felt sweaty as I lifted the receiver. "Hello?" I said in a shaky voice.

"Solano."

My hope crashed through the floorboards. "Yeah. Hi, Max."

"Today. Two o'clock. Peacemobile."

I exhaled wearily. "I don't know —"

"Be there." The phone buzzed in my ear.

Hey, who was the leader of the Snob Squad, anyway? Right, Jenny, I answered myself. I couldn't even take charge of my own life.

"Good morning, sweetheart." Mom came in from the living room. She kissed me on the cheek.

What was *her* problem?

"How was your date?" she asked.

"Short," I said.

"Oh?" She cocked her head. "Is there something you want to tell me?"

Like what? I thought. You gave birth to a loser? "No," I answered.

Dad moseyed in from the hallway. Setting the laundry basket on the basement landing, he refilled his coffee cup and said, "I made cinnamon rolls for breakfast, which the rest of us finished three hours ago."

My eyes flickered up to the kitchen clock. Holy moly, it was almost noon. Usually I slept late on weekends, but not past *Xena: Warrior Princess*. Today I just wanted to go back to bed, for like forever.

"Something happened last night during Jenny's

date," Mom said to Dad. They exchanged knowing glances, although I wasn't sure what they knew.

Dad said, "Did he put the moves on you?"

"Robert!" Mom whapped him. To me, she said, "Did he?"

"Don't I wish," I mumbled.

Dad said, "He loves her, he loves her, he loves her." He wiggled his eyebrows.

I looked at him funny. He was definitely losing it. In a sigh, I said, "Where's Vanessa?"

"At orchestra rehearsal," Mom said. "For the Young Performers concert tomorrow night. Which reminds me, you'll need to find a nice outfit to wear. Preferably something hanging in your closet, as opposed to on the floor. If you need anything washed, you'd better get it downstairs."

I tuned Mom out around the word *tomorrow*. For me, there was no tomorrow. I did feel bad about the way I'd snapped at Vanessa last night and wanted to apologize. Especially since it might be my last act on Earth.

Mom stopped me on the way back to my room. "Jenny," she said, "does this have anything to do with that stolen money? Were you right? Did Kevin steal it to buy you those presents?"

All I could do was shake my head. I didn't even finish the shake before it struck me. "How'd you know about that?"

Mom looked at Dad. Neither one answered.

"I'll kill her!" I cried. Clenching both fists, I screamed at the ceiling, "Vanessa, you snoop!" I charged down the hall and into her room. I didn't know what I was looking for. Something personal, something to trash. Vanessa had been in my room. She'd been reading my food diary. Even worse, she'd shared it with Mom and Dad.

The first thing I stumbled into was her music stand. As it toppled over, pages of sheet music fluttered to the floor. Without thinking, I grabbed one up and ripped it in half.

"Jenny!" Mom yanked at my hand. "What are you doing?"

"She invaded my privacy," I said. "I'm going to kill her." In a twisting motion, I wrenched away from Mom. As I started to tear the next sheet of music, tears pooled in my eyes. How could she? My own sister. And she had the gall to make me feel guilty about not trusting her last night. Ooh!

"Jenny, stop it!" Hands grabbed my shoulders and spun me around. "Vanessa wasn't in your room. I was. I read your diary."

Through heavy tears, I blinked up. My fuzzy vision cleared. I had to blink again. I couldn't believe it. "Dad?"

Chapter 23

Dad held up both hands. "I confess," he said. "I know I shouldn't have, but your notebook was sitting there on your pillow. It looked like a school report or something. I just went in to change your sheets because I forgot to tell you girls that I was moving the wash day for sheets and towels from Tuesday to Friday."

An echo sounded in my head. He loves her, he loves her — oh, my God. He'd read that far?

My eyes blinked over to Mom. She smiled meekly and said, "Your father told me about it last night. If I'd known, I never would've let you go out with that boy." She shot eye daggers at Dad.

He sniped at her, "I told you I was sorry. I thought it was Jenny's business, not ours."

Mom huffed. She said to me, "I agree it was wrong of your father to read your diary, but really, Jenny.

Some of the stuff in there is serious. Is it true, about the stolen money?"

I blinked back to Dad. "You read my diary?"

"I didn't know. Okay, I figured it out and probably should've stopped. But then I got to the part about the money and . . ." He shrugged.

"You read my diary," I said again. "You broke into my room and read my diary."

"I didn't *break* in." He widened his eyes at me. "It was time to change the bedding and —"

I stiff-armed my way between them.

"Jenny, your father wasn't invading your privacy. He — we — would never do that."

At Vanessa's door I stopped and spun. "As of this moment, you are no longer my parents. I divorce you." With that, I slammed the door in their faces.

All the way to Max's house, I fumed. How could they? How could *he?* And how could *she* support him? They always taught us to respect each other's privacy. We weren't even allowed to enter each other's rooms without knocking; without verbal permission. When did the rules change? When did my privacy become less important than theirs?

Tears streamed down my cheeks. I'd never forgive him. Never. The three-mile walk to Max's was a blur.

I was so angry and hurt and hollow. Losing Kevin wasn't enough; now I'd lost my family.

Thank God for the Snob Squad, I thought. At least my friends were true blue.

When I arrived at the Peacemobile, Max and Prairie were already there. "Hey," I mumbled, hauling myself up into the minivan. I flopped onto the flowered sofa in my usual spot. "Don't ask me for any money because I won't be inheriting the family fortune. I just divorced my parents."

Neither of them spoke. I glanced up. They both glared at me, with something like hatred in their eyes.

"What?" I said.

Max broke her glare and stared up over my head. "Where's Lyd?" she said.

"How should I know?" I answered. "Probably at ballet. Probably her mother is picking her up and bringing her here because she has a mother she loves and trusts."

They still didn't ask. What did I have to do, slit my belly open and spill my guts all over the floor?

Prairie just sat and stared at me. She's still mad about last night, I thought. Okay, it was my fault the date ended early. So report me to the date police.

The silence was staggering. I hated knowing Prairie was mad at me. Just as I opened my mouth to apologize for the hundredth time, the door to the

Peacemobile slid open and Lydia climbed in. "What's the emergency?" she said. Her eyes darted around. They stopped on me. A frown furrowed her brow. "Jenny, what's wrong?"

Well, finally! Someone who cared. "My father's been sneaking into my room and reading my diary," I told her.

"You keep a diary?" Lydia asked. "Don't you lock it?"

"No," I said. "I mean, it's my food diary. It didn't come with a key."

Lydia slid in beside me. "So, what's to see in your food diary?"

"It's more than that. I was writing a bunch of personal stuff, too."

Behind her glasses, Lydia's eyes magnified. "How personal?"

"Very personal."

"Like how you accused Kevin of stealing Mrs. Jonas's and Ms. Milner's money?" Prairie piped up.

My face flared. "I never accused him," I said. "I only mentioned that it was a coincidence about the money and my presents. And I mean, come on. He's going to spend his own money on me? Where did he get that much money? It's obvious he isn't rich."

Prairie exhaled exasperation. She shook her head.

"When was this?" Lydia twisted to face me.

I heaved a heavy sigh. "Last night."

"At your date?"

"Yes!" I snapped at her.

Lydia's jaw dropped.

"I only asked him if he did it. I never accused him."

"Same difference," Lydia said.

Oh, thanks a lot, I thought.

Max asked, "So, what did he say?"

I looked at her. "What would *you* say?"

She shrugged.

"Really, Max." I shifted my weight to face her. "If I asked whether you took Mrs. Jonas's and Ms. Milner's money, what would you say?"

Her face darkened. "Do you think I did?"

I threw up my hands. "That's just what Kevin said. Right before he threw me out of his house. And his life." A lump lodged in my throat.

Suddenly it grew deathly quiet. Prairie and Max both had the same look of contempt on their faces that Kevin had carved forever in my memory. "What?" I barked at them.

Max's eyes dropped and she slugged down a Coke. Prairie kept staring. To her I added, "Didn't you for a minute suspect Hugh?"

"Hugh?" Her voice rose. "N-no way."

Now I really felt like a dirtball. I'd managed to

alienate everyone: my sister, my boyfriend, my friends. And I was still no closer to the truth.

My gaze flickered back to Max. I decided to risk it. What else did I have to lose? "So, Max, you never told us where you got the money for your shoes and the new CD player."

Max said, "You never asked."

I could scream. Maybe I did. Then I said, "Well, now I'm asking."

She took another long swig of Coke. "My brother sold this guy a rebuilt Harley. A classic, the guy said. And since I helped rebuild the engine, I got half the money."

"See?" I looked around. "All you have to do is tell the truth." I sat back, arms folded, feeling satisfied. The satisfaction faded to guilt. How could I have suspected Max? And since I knew she was telling the truth, it meant Kevin... My arms dropped. My whole body sagged.

"Yeah, Jenny," Prairie broke into my misery. "So why don't you?"

I frowned. "Why don't I what?"

Max crushed the Coke can in her hand. "Come on, Solano. We know you did it. Fess up."

Did wha—?" I choked. I knew what. "You think I stole that money?"

Max scooted forward in the beanbag chair, leaning

toward me. "It's okay," she said. "We don't know why you did it, but you must've had a good reason."

"Me?" I slapped my chest. It hurt, or else my heart was bruised.

Prairie took my hand and held it between hers. "You can tell us, Jenny."

"No," I said to her, withdrawing my hand. "I can't."

Prairie cocked her head. "That's why I returned the money. As much as I could, anyway. I didn't know you already gave it back. I'm sorry." Her eyes lowered. "I should've trusted you to do the r-right thing."

"You gave the money back?" Max's gaze shifted to Prairie. "But I sold my CD player —"

Prairie gasped. She covered her mouth with both hands. "You really *did* use that m-money for the starving orphans? Why didn't you tell me?"

Max said, "You never asked."

"Wait a minute, wait a minute." My mind was racing a million miles a second. Not only did they think I did it, they returned the money they thought I stole. All three of them? I looked at Lydia. I wasn't sure if I should hate them or love them. "I didn't do it," I said. "You guys. Why did you think *I* stole the money? How *could* you think it?"

Prairie's eyes met mine, searching. Her brow furrowed. "That day Mrs. Jonas's money got stolen, you were in her desk."

"I was not! Kevin was getting chalk so we could play hangman. He snitched a few M&M's —" I stopped. A chill raced up my spine and I banished the memory. "You and Hugh were up there, too," I countered. "What were you doing?"

Prairie's cheeks turned pink. "Just t-talking," she said. "Anyway," she hurried on, "you knew how much money was stolen. And you and Kevin were with me and Hugh in the lab that day after lunch to see the snake. And, I, uh, saw you looking in Ms. Milner's desk drawer."

Heat fried my face. "She had a box of Little Debbie snack cakes in there. Do you know how long it's been since I've had a Little Debbie? Okay, I admit, I was tempted to take one. But I didn't! And for sure I didn't take any money."

Max continued, "Then that day at the mall you had money for batteries and lunch —"

"My dad gave me twenty bucks to buy him boxer shorts."

Everyone looked at me then.

"I swear to God!" I crossed my heart. "You guys. I wouldn't do something like that. I'm not a thief. Come on, you know me." Or did they? Like Max said, do you ever really know another person?

How could I prove my innocence? I couldn't, except . . . "What did you think I spent the money on?"

Max's intense stare at my neck was the answer.

"The presents from Kevin? Prairie, you heard Hugh and Kevin talking about the earrings. And Lydia," I said, twisting around to face her, "you saw Kevin give me the necklace."

Lydia nodded.

I turned back, folding my arms in a huff. "There." I felt angry, offended, crushed. Tears filled my eyes. How could they think I'd done it? What kind of person did they think I was?

I felt Prairie's eyes on me, boring into me. "Jenny," she said softly. "Is that the truth?"

Sniffling, I looked at her and said, "Yes."

A long, excruciating moment went by, as if judgment was being passed. Then Prairie drew back. Slowly, her hands rose to cover her mouth again. "Oh, Jenny," she said. "I'm so s-sorry."

I blinked up at Max. She seemed stunned, like this whole scene was surreal. Which it was. Swallowing hard, I said, "I'm sorry, too. For thinking you did it, Max."

Her eyes widened briefly, then burned bullet holes in my head.

"I didn't want to believe it," I told her. "But the shoes and the CD player . . ." It was all I could say. If Max was going to pound me into pulp, she should do it now.

180

Instead, she growled, "I guess I understand. I know I have a rep, and I have done some bad stuff, okay? I never said I was an angel. I might've lifted a few things at the mall." She added hastily, "But that was before. And I never took nothin' from a teacher."

We were quiet for a long minute, letting the air clear between us. I looked from Max to Prairie to Lydia. Well, at least that solved the mystery of the three Good Samaritans. Even though they did it to cover for me, I didn't feel much better. Finally Prairie said, "If you didn't do it and Max didn't do it, then the only other person is Ashley."

"Not necessarily." As I opened my mouth to speak his name, probably for the last time, a whoosh of air caught my breath. The sofa jerked as Lydia jumped to her feet. "Okay." She threw up her arms. "You can stop torturing me. I confess. I did it."

Chapter 24

All eyes glommed onto Lydia's face. Mine had to be stuck the hardest. Lydia gulped. "I didn't mean to take the money," she said. "It just happened."

My jaw unhinged. Mine wasn't the only one. "You're going to have to do better than that, Lydia," I informed her.

She glanced down at me, looking scared. My tone of voice startled me. But if she was telling the truth . . .

Lydia's knees collapsed and she dropped back down to the sofa. Her head fell against the back springs as she closed her eyes. "Remember that day when I went in before school to fix my diorama? That's when it happened."

"When what happened?" I asked.

Lydia opened her eyes and said, "When I stole Mrs. Jonas's money."

"Geez, Lydia. I knew you were mad at her, but —"

She cut me off. "It wasn't just that. I mean, okay, that was part of it. I've reported Ashley to her a hundred times for breaking the rules and Mrs. Jonas never does anything about it. And you know Ashley's been on my case all year. So then that day, Ashley and Melanie were playing around with my diorama, laughing and making jokes about it, and Mrs. Jonas just expected me to just blow it off and help them. And I thought, Here I am getting punished and having to do extra work for something Ashley did."

We all exchanged nods. She was right. It wasn't fair. But that was no excuse for stealing.

"Anyway." Lydia drew a deep breath. "Mrs. Jonas got called to the office and I needed her Wite-Out to paint those stupid mustaches off the Founding Fathers, and when I got to her desk the drawer was open and her purse was sitting there with an envelope full of money. Ashley and Melanie had gone to the bathroom to . . ." Lydia paused and blanched. "Whatever it is they do in there, and it all just made me so mad and I, I, reached in and took the money." She was breathing hard. At any moment, she was going to have an asthma attack. Turning to face me, she added, "I didn't mean to do it. It was just this urge I couldn't control. You know?"

Unfortunately, I did. I had to fight the same demon urge every time I saw a Snickers bar. I might've nodded.

Lydia said, "I know it was a bad thing to do. But later, it seemed to be the perfect opportunity to catch Ashley in the act. Like you said we had to, Jenny."

"Me?" All the blood rushed to my face. "When did I say that?"

"Here, in the Peacemobile," she answered. "That day we were trying to figure out how to get Ashley."

"Hey, don't put this off on me. I never meant —"

Max jumped in. "So, how does your stealing money catch Krupps in the act?"

"Good question." I looked at Lydia.

She clucked. "I was going to put the stolen money in Ashley's purse. But, as you know, she sleeps with that stupid purse."

"Let me get this straight." I backed away from Lydia so that I could face her head-on. So that I could put some distance between us. Before I could formulate a question, though, Prairie asked, "Did you steal Ms. M-Milner's money, too?"

Lydia let out a short laugh. "Okay, let me explain."

"You did?" I may have spit on her. "Lydia —"

"I did it for Max," she said.

Max's eyes about popped out of their sockets. We were all so flabbergasted, no one could speak. Lydia sobered fast and added, "When I was hiding from the snake back there and saw the money, the perfect plan came to me. I could kill two birds with one stone. Since Max was suspended, she couldn't get blamed. And if I could somehow plant the money on Ashley . . ." Lydia aimed an accusing finger at Max. "Then *you* had to go ruin it by showing up at school. What were you doing there, anyway?"

Max curled a lip. "I left my Nikes in my gym locker. Is that a crime?"

Compared to Lydia's felonious activities, I thought not.

"Let me get this straight," I started again. "You stole the money so you could clear Max's name and frame Ashley?"

"Exactly." Lydia pointed her finger at me. "I mean, no." She dropped her arm. "I didn't *mean* to steal the money. It wasn't premeditated or anything. But it was sort of like fate. It's what we always wanted, right? To get Ashley?"

"Yeah," I said. "To get her for something she's done. Geez, Lydia." I shook my head. "I don't know which is worse. Stealing the money or framing an innocent person."

"Ashley Krupps is not innocent." Lydia's voice rose. "She's guilty as sin."

"Stealing is the sin," Prairie said softly.

Lydia's eyes flickered over to her. "I know. I know it was wrong. I was sorry the minute I took the money. I've never done anything like that in my whole life. And as soon as you told us what Ms. Milner's money was for, I put it back."

"What about Mrs. Jonas's money?" I asked. "If you're so sorry, why didn't you give hers back, too?"

Lydia's face fell. "I couldn't," she mumbled. She folded her hands in her lap. "I spent it."

"On what?" we all said together.

Lydia swallowed hard. In a tiny voice, she answered, "On earrings like yours and Prairie's. Because I don't have a boyfriend to give me expensive presents. And I never will." She burst into tears.

Prairie and I looked hopelessly at one another. Prairie searched in her pack for a Kleenex and handed it to Lydia. A vision materialized in my head. The gray velvet box. "Were those the earrings —"

I didn't even get to finish before Lydia nodded violently. "Now Ashley has *them*, too," she wailed.

Lydia sobbed and wheezed at the same time. It was a heart-wrenching sound, especially right in my ear. Prairie was the one who went over to Lydia. Straddling the sofa arm, she patted Lydia's back and said, "It's okay, Lyd."

"No, it's not." Lydia hiccuped. "I'm a horrible person."

The three of us looked at each other. It's at a moment like this you start to remember all the bad things you've done in your life. Like hoarding food in your room and lying about it. Like sneaking into your sister's room and exchanging your old Michael Jackson CD for her new NSYNC. Like copying off Lydia's science quizzes all year. Like accusing your boyfriend of being a crook.

I slid over closer to Lydia and patted her other shoulder blade. "Look, Lydia," I said. "No one's perfect. I just wish you'd told us sooner so we wouldn't have suspected each other."

"I tried," Lydia snuffled. "But all you and Prairie ever wanted to talk about was your stupid boyfriends."

Was that true? Prairie met my eyes. Wow, had we made Lydia and Max feel left out? I looked at Max. She shrugged, as if she didn't care. But then, Max was a different person from Lydia.

Lydia blew her nose. "Buying the earrings was the dumbest thing I ever did," she blubbered. "I couldn't even wear them. You guys would notice and my mom would want to know where I got them. You hate me now, don't you? You're going to kick me off the Squad. And I wouldn't blame you."

Before she suffered an irreversible emotional breakdown, I said, "We don't hate you, Lydia. We can't. It's against the Snob Squad rules."

She blinked at me.

"All for one and one for all?" I did the Snob Squad salute.

That brought a weak smile to Lydia's tortured face. A horn honked out front and we all started. It was Lydia's mother coming to pick her up.

"Oh, my God!" Lydia freaked. "She's going to kill me when she finds out what I did."

"So don't tell her," Max said.

Lydia scoffed. "I have to tell her. She's my mother. Anyway, I have to get Mrs. Jonas's money back to her somehow." She blew her nose. "Unless you guys have a plan."

Before we could respond, she shook her head and said, "Forget that. This is my problem. It's something I have to fix myself."

I'm glad she realized that. Even if we could figure out a way to raise eighty-five dollars, Lydia would still have to tell her mother. She knew it, and we knew it.

We all got up at once. Sliding open the minivan door, I advised her, "Just tell your mom exactly what you told us. Try to slip in the fact that she's the one who forced you to solve your own problems without her help."

Everyone arched eyebrows at me.

"Hey, it never hurts to lay a little guilt trip on them."

Max caught Lydia's arm. "You want me to go with you? So your mom doesn't beat you bloody or nothin'?"

Lydia sneered at Max. "My mother doesn't beat me. She's a child psychologist. Duh."

"Uh, one suggestion," I said to Lydia. "Don't remind her of that just now."

The horn honked again. Lydia flinched. She inhaled a deep breath and, stepping down from the van, said, "Well, here goes. It's been fun. If I never see you guys again . . ."

"You'll see us again," I assured her. "You can't get rid of us that easily." As she disappeared into the weeds, I hollered at her back, "I'll call you tonight."

Lydia turned. "Don't call after nine. You'll get me in trouble."

Which cracked me up, for some reason. Cracked us all up, even Lydia. Prairie slipped an arm around my waist and one around Max's. We shared this silent understanding. About friendship and what it meant. Like forgiveness and trust and loyalty. Being there for each other in times of need, through thick or thin. In Lydia's case, extra thick.

Chapter 25

Dear Faith in Friends but Furious at My Father Food Diary,

It makes sense now, why Lydia's been acting so weird, so mad all the time. Guilt will do that to a person; eat away at you until you can't even stand yourself. Especially if you're a good person, deep down, the way I know Lydia is.

I stopped writing and sighed sadly. Poor Lydia. With one impulsive act, she'd ruined her life. Ruined mine, too.

"Oh, that isn't true," I said out loud. Her life wasn't over. It just wasn't going to be much fun for a while. In my food diary I wrote,

No one can ruin your life except you. And I sure ruined it with Kevin. I thought about calling him or writing him a letter of apology, but how do

*you apologize for not trusting someone you love?
Like Dad.*

*I still can't get over what Dad did. I'll never
forgive him.*

I paused again and shook my head. Flipping to the
next page, I continued at the top,

*That isn't true, either. I have to forgive him,
he's my dad. If I'm not forgiving, how can I expect others to be? Guess what else, dear diary? I
lost two and a half pounds in two weeks. And it
doesn't even matter.*

"Jenny, breakfast," Dad hollered down the hall.

When I didn't break down the door to get to the
kitchen, I guess he got concerned. A minute later a
knock sounded.

"Jenny?"

"What?" I snapped. Hey, I said I'd forgive him, not
make his life easy.

"Can I come in?"

"Just a minute. Let me hide my valuables." Slowly
I moved toward the door. Ten, twenty, thirty seconds
passed. Opening the door a crack, I asked, "Yes?"

"Come to breakfast," he said. "We're celebrating
the first day of summer vacation."

I didn't feel like there was much to celebrate. Not even the fact that I could finally wear shorts, since Kevin would never see me in the flesh.

"I made waffles." Dad wiggled his eyebrows. "With blueberry syrup and Cool Whip."

"I'm not all that hungry," I lied. Could he detect my hyperventilating? If he thought the way to my heart was through my stomach, he was right. I opened the door.

"I am sorry, Jenny," Dad said before I could brush by him. "I didn't mean to hurt you. And I promise never to come in your room again without your permission."

"Stop it," I said. "You're making me misty." Which he was.

He clamped a hand over my shoulder. "Forgive me?"

I shrugged. "Can I put a lock on my door?"

"No," he said.

It was worth a try.

"But your mom and I decided to put in another phone. Maybe here at the end of the hall so you and Vanessa can share it."

"Really?" My heart soared. "All right!" Then my spirits sank. It was too late. Now there was no one to hold a deeply private conversation with.

Vanessa and Mom were already sitting at the table,

chatting away. As I slid in, Vanessa said to Mom, "Is that what you guys were whispering about behind my back at putt-putt? Geez, Dad." She glared at him.

Mom and Dad both looked sheepish.

Van said to me, "I can't believe it. If he ever did that to me, I'd disown him."

Dad slithered into his chair.

"I'm sorry about ripping up your music," I told her. "For a minute, I thought you were the snoop."

"Yeah, Mom told me that, too. Don't worry about it; I already had that piece memorized."

Dad said, "Could we put this behind us and move on?"

I decided to twist the knife. "He's pleading temporary insanity, Van. What do you think?"

Vanessa looked him over. "Why temporary?"

"Good question," I said. "It must be true, though, because did you hear, he's going to buy us a phone?"

"What?" Her jaw unhinged. "Awesome." She smiled. Spreading Cool Whip over her waffle, her smile vanished and she added, "Like anyone would ever call me."

"Yeah, me either." I plopped a waffle on my plate.

Van met my eyes. I sighed and answered her unspoken question. "We broke up."

Everyone kept eating, not looking up. Trying, I guess, not to press on my one big bruise, inside and out. It didn't work. "Don't you want to know what happened?" I asked.

In unison they all said, "Yes."

Mom added, "If you want to tell us."

So, even though they probably knew most of it, I began at the beginning. I told them about Mrs. Jonas and the stolen money. About Ms. Milner's money and the starving orphans in India. About how the presents from Kevin coincided with the thefts, so that I thought he'd done it. Same with the circumstantial evidence against Max. Then how Max and Prairie thought *I'd* done it, and covered my butt by returning Ms. Milner's money. I told them almost everything, except the part about losing weight. Some things really are private.

The horror story held them rapt, especially when I got to the part about Lydia confessing. They couldn't believe it.

"So Ms. Milner got all her money back?" Mom said, refilling her cup of coffee.

"And more. Like three times as much."

"And what about Mrs. Jonas?"

Yes, Mrs. Jonas. "Well, when I called Lydia last night, she said she and her mom were still talking. They were going to figure out a way to pay Mrs. Jonas back for everything." Knowing Lydia's mom, it was going to cost more than eighty-five dollars. More than money. This expression Lydia had used came back to me: Two more weeks of total living hell. I wanted Lydia to know that if she got grounded for life, we could always move the Snob Squad headquarters to her house.

Even though Lydia kept sniffling and blowing her nose, the relief in her voice was evident. It's like Oprah says: Confession is good for the soul.

"Unbelievable," Vanessa said. "It's always the person you least suspect."

"Tell me about it," I replied. My eyes met Dad's. His drilled a hole in the tabletop. "It's a good thing Lydia told her mom herself because you know how this kind of stuff gets out. It's like nothing we ever do is a secret from our parents."

"Oh, Jenny," Mom said.

"I'm not keeping secrets from you," I informed her, and Dad. "It's just that some stuff is personal. And private."

"That's the truth." Vanessa folded her napkin in her lap.

"I know that," Mom said. "Your father and I have been discussing this with Dr. Sid, too. We all have private lives, and we shouldn't expect you to share everything with us."

That sounded like Dr. Sid. But why did it take a trained professional to tell them something so obvious? Maybe it wasn't obvious. Maybe I had a career ahead of me in psychology.

Mom reached over for Dad's hand. "We'd just like you girls to know we're here for you, if you need us."

Vanessa's eyes met mine. "We know that," we said together.

It was like Disney, this magic moment. Except rather than the four of us bursting into song, the doorbell sang.

"Criminetly, who's that?" Dad grumbled. He scootched back his chair and stood. "If it's another Bible thumper, they're going to find out what a real thumping is."

"Ooh, scary," I said to Van. We both faked shudders.

"You want the last waffle, Jenny?" Mom asked, passing me the plate.

"No, thanks," I said. "I'm watching my weight."

Mom dropped her jaw. Well, geez. Why did she think I was keeping a food diary?

Dad appeared in the doorway. "You have a visitor," he said.

When I looked up to see who he meant, I gulped a grapefruit. My fork fell out of my hand and clattered to the floor.

"Hey, Jen," Kevin said.

Chapter 26

"I can't stay long because my mom and I are on our way to Utah to visit my grandma and grandpa. But I wanted to tell you something before I left."

Three sets of blood-sucking eyes from the living-room window attached themselves to Kevin and me on the porch. Before I could suggest we go for a walk, or a run, Kevin sat on the front stoop.

I sank down beside him. Slowly, so he wouldn't see my legs jiggle to a stop. He was already giving off weird vibes. "So, how are you?" he asked.

"I've been better," I answered.

He looked at me, then away. It confirmed what I already knew. The only reason Kevin would come by was to get his gifts back.

"I'm sorry about Saturday night," he said. "I was a jerk."

My eyes bounced off the concrete.

"After I thought about what you said, I could see how you might've put two and two together."

"And come up with five," I muttered.

He chuckled. Sobering fast, he added, "I took out some money from my savings to buy you that stuff. And my aunt Rachel paid me for helping her move. And" — he lowered his head and his voice — "the necklace didn't cost ninety-five dollars. I just put it in a box I found in the garage. I didn't steal anything from anybody."

My ears burned. My whole insides felt like they were on fire. "I know you didn't, Kevin," I said. "I'm sorry I accused you. It was stupid. I don't want you to think I don't trust you."

"Do you?" He stared into my eyes. Real hard, like he was trying to look deep down inside.

"Yes," I said. "And that's the honest truth."

He exhaled a long sigh. "I don't know who took that money, but it wasn't me. In fact, I put some of Ms. Milner's money back. As much as I could. I left an IOU for the rest. For the starving orphans in India . . ." He shook his head. "I saw those pictures in her room."

At that moment I fell in love with Kevin Rooney all over again. In unison, we both asked the same question: "Do you forgive me?"

It cracked us up. Kevin added, "I can't believe I acted like such a jerk."

"Me, neither," I said.

He drew back from me.

I added quickly, "I mean, I can't believe *I* was a jerk. For suspecting you."

That made us laugh again, even though it wasn't really funny. Without warning, Kevin leapt to his feet. I scrambled up after him. He reached over and took my hand. The feel of his skin against mine sent a tingle up my arm. Then he took my other hand, and the tingle extended to the tips of my toes. "I'm going to be gone for like three weeks." He made a face. "But I'll call you, okay?"

From Utah? Where is Utah? I wondered. Then I thought, Who cares? It's long distance. He's going to call *me* long distance.

"I'll call you every day," he said. Without warning, he leaned forward and kissed me.

I can't tell you how long the kiss lasted because I lost consciousness. When my eyes opened, I was surprised to find myself still standing. I could've sworn I'd blasted into space.

Kevin smiled at me. His cheeks were all red. "See you, Jen," he said.

Just like that. See you, Jen. It held promise.

As he sprinted down the sidewalk and up the street out of sight, blood began to flow through my veins again. In my peripheral vision, I caught a movement in the front picture window. The curtains fell back into place. Oh, great. So much for privacy.

I slammed through the front door, screaming, "When can we get that phone?"

Dear Dreaming of Delicious Days and Freedom from Diet Food Forever Diary,

I can't wait to tell you what I did on my summer vacation. As soon as it happens, you'll be the first to know.

They say love is blind, but I don't believe it. I think love gives you something like X-ray vision, so you can see beneath the surface to what's deep down inside.

And that's the truth, the whole truth, and nothing but the truth.